islam

# islam

## CLAIRE ALKOUATLI

*Many thanks to those who have guided me along the way starting with my mother and father, my uncle in Dhaka, my first teacher, my teacher who knows his students, and, most of all, the guide behind all guides. Thanks beyond words go to my beloved husband. My efforts are dedicated to my baby, who was born during the writing of this book. May he lead a generation better than ours.*

Marshall Cavendish Benchmark • 99 White Plains Road • Tarrytown, NY 10591-9001 • www.marshallcavendish.us

All Internet sites were available and accurate when the book was sent to press. • Library of Congress Cataloging-in-Publication Data • Alkouatli, Claire. • Islam / by Claire Alkouatli.— 1st ed. • p. cm. — (World religions) • Summary: "Provides an overiew of the history and origins, basic tenets and beliefs, organization, traditions, customs, rites, societal and historical influences, and modern-day impact of Islam"—Provided by publisher. • Includes bibliographical references and index. • ISBN-13: 978-0-7614-2120-7 • ISBN-10: 0-7614-2120-3 • 1. Islam—Juvenile literature. I. Title. II. Series: World religions • (Marshall Cavendish Benchmark) • BP161.3.A425 2006 • 297—dc22 • 2005026862 • Series design by Sonia Chaghatzbanian • Photo research by Candlepants Incorporated • Cover photo: J.B.Russell/SYGMA / Corbis • The photographs in this book are used by permission and through the courtesy of:

*Corbis*: David Sutherland, 1, 3, back cover; Suhaib Salem/Reuters, 2, 4-5, 6-7; Jon Spall, 8; Adnan Abidi/Reuters, 31, 33, 66, 79, 92, 96, 109; Michael S. Yamashita, 40; J. Raga/zefa, 51; Dwi Oblo/Reuters, 60; Ali Abbas/epa, 81, 97; Ali Haider/epa, 89; Martin Harvey, 93; Reuters, 100; Finbarr O'Reilly/Reuters, 103; Peter Beck, 108. *Super Stock*: age footstock, 14; Brand X, 27; PhotoAlto, 76. *Art Resource, NY*: Werner Forman, 49. *Art Archive*: HarperCollins Publishers, 83.

Printed in China • 1 3 5 6 4 2

# c o n t e n t s

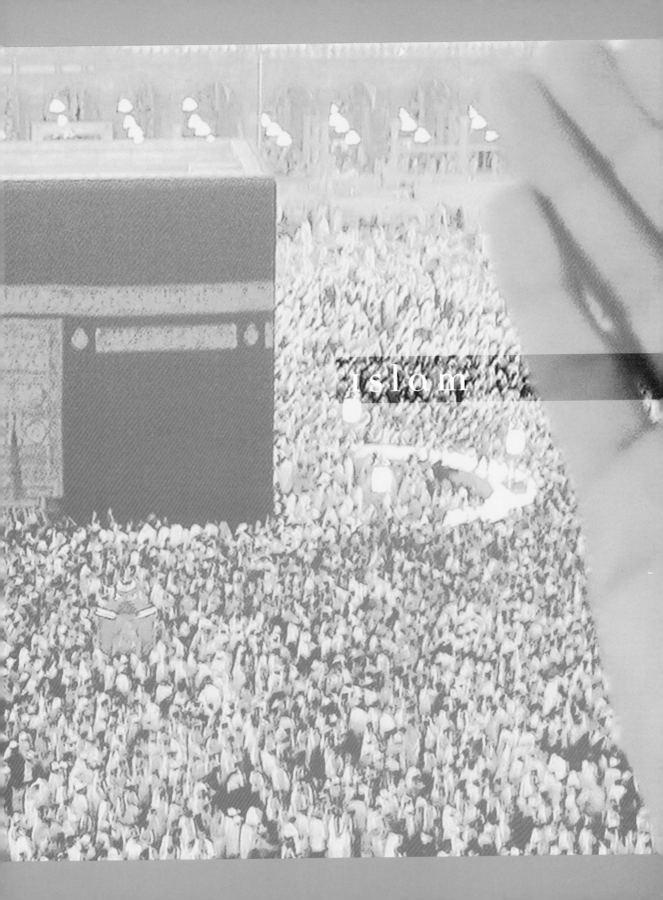

A group of women walks by the ornately styled Tomb of Ali, also known as the Blue Mosque, in Mazari-i-Sharif, Afghanistan.

# JOURNEY TO ISLAM

## The first muslims

A few thousand years ago, in the middle of the Arabian Peninsula, a man by the name of Abraham left his wife and their young son Ishmael in a barren valley. The three had been traveling for more than a month and provisions were slim by the time they reached the desert valley where Abraham bid his family farewell and turned to leave.

His wife, Hagar, called out to his retreating back, "Abraham! Are you just going to leave us here?"

Abraham didn't answer; he just kept walking.

Hagar called out to him again, "Who will protect us?"

Again, he didn't answer.

Hagar asked her final question: "Is this a Divine command?"

Abraham turned to her and replied, "Yes."

Hagar, satisfied at last, said, "Then God will keep us safe."

Soon Hagar and Ishmael's supplies dwindled, and they became thirsty. Ishmael started wailing for water, kicking his feet in the sand, so Hagar ascended a nearby hill to have a look around. All she saw were desolate mountains and the shimmering sand of the valley floor. So she ascended another hill and looked around again. Seven times, in increasing desperation, Hagar moved between these two hills looking for water until she glanced back at her son and saw that a spring had gushed up under his flailing heels.

This spring became the well called Zamzam. Gradually a settlement of people grew up around it, and eventually the settlement became the town called Mecca. Abraham later returned and with Ishmael built a sanctuary for the worship of God called the Ka'bah. Time passed and Mecca grew to be an important trading and pilgrimage town.

Abraham is known as the forefather of the three great monotheistic faiths—Judaism, Christianity, and Islam—because of his unswerving devotion to one God. When he was less than sixteen years old, he argued with his father, a sculptor of idols, saying, "How can you worship that which your own hands create?" When his polytheistic people threw him into a great fire to burn him for his beliefs, he repeated the refrain, "God is sufficient for me and the best trustee. I don't need anyone or anything but God." When Muslims recount this story, they ask: "Are the laws of nature binding on the One who created them? God made the sea split for Moses, diseases vanish for Jesus, and the fire cool for Abraham." Abraham walked out of that great fire unscathed.

Later, when traveling through a culture of people who worshipped stars and planets, Abraham stood out on the field with them and selected the planet Venus as his god. When Venus set, he said, "I don't worship those that set. I turn my face towards the One who crafted the heavens and the earth . . ." (Quran 6:76 and 6:79)

Jews and Christians hail from Abraham's son Isaac, and Muslims from that son he left in the desert, Ishmael. The story of Ishmael and Hagar in the desert illustrates the essence of the Islamic faith, which is surrender. When Abraham left them, he was surrendering to a divine command. Hagar, in accepting this situation, was also surrendering. She knew that her well-being did not ultimately lie with Abraham—or anyone else. She put her trust in God.

The word *Islam* literally means "to surrender" in Arabic. The word also connotes peace. Muslims are people who submit themselves to God. Abraham and his family, according to Islamic sources, were the first to be called Muslims.

To this day, Zamzam continues to gush pure water, quenching the thirst of the millions of people who go on pilgrimages every year to Mecca, now known as the City of Honor.

## In a cave called Hira

Fast-forward some two thousand years to the year 610. Mecca had grown into an important city situated on the spice route between Africa and Asia; merchants there traded in goods brought from Zanzibar and Abyssinia in Africa and from the cities of the north and the east such as Cairo, Aqaba, and Damascus. At that time, the people of Mecca were grouped into tribes that feuded with one another over issues such as water, land, and the right to oversee the holy shrine of the Ka'bah built by Abraham and Ishmael. But the days of Abraham and his message of monotheism had been lost, and now people worshiped a great number of gods whose idols were housed in the Ka'bah. Muslims today call this period *jahiliyyah,* or the age of ignorance.

Out of this polytheistic setting emerged a man called Muhammad. He often took to the mountains surrounding Mecca for spiritual retreat. In Hira, a rocky cave high above the town, Muhammad sat quietly. A bright light appeared, and a thundering voice filled the cave commanding Muhammad: "Read!"

"But I cannot read!" whispered a surprised Muhammad. He could neither read nor write.

"Read!" again came the command.

Then Muhammad felt himself being compressed in an unbearable embrace, and an awesome presence—the angel Gabriel—recited to Muhammad these lines:

**Read in the name of your Lord,**
**Who has created the human being from a fusion clot!**
**Read, for most gentle and bountiful is your Lord,**

**The One who has taught man the use of a pen,
Taught man what he knew not."** *(Quran 96:1–5)*

The *Quran*, an Arabic word meaning "recitation," is the holy book of the Islamic faith. The verses that were revealed to Muhammad over the course of two decades lie at the heart of Islam. The events of Muhammad's life are examples and illuminations of the messages contained within the Quran.

The Quran is considered by Muslims to be the literal speech of God, a recital where stories, laws, and divine insights intertwine with lyric and rhythm. Muslims consider the sunset and starscape and the most beautiful sights in the natural world to be like the pages of the Quran—they all come from the same divine source.

The angel Gabriel told Muhammad that he was to be a messenger of God, a prophet whose mission was to shake his people out of their immoral stupor and polytheistic orientation and re-establish the religion of his forefather Abraham.

According to Islamic tradition, Muhammad was a direct descendent of Abraham, through Ishmael, although the two were separated by more than two thousand years (scholars guess that Abraham likely lived around 2000 B.C.E.). Muhammad and Abraham were also linked by Mecca—the place where Muhammad lived and received his revelations had been established by Hagar and Ishmael. Finally, the two prophets were linked by the message itself.

This message of monotheism and human morality, responsibility, and equality was not for Muhammad's culture and time period only. Muslims believe that Muhammad's message was intended for all people, at all times, because it is a reiteration of the messages of past prophets and messengers such as Abraham, Jesus, Moses, Noah, and Jacob, to list a few of the twenty-five who are named in the Quran.

At the center of the message is the One, that transcendent and absolute power known as the Truth, the Divine, the Real, or Allah, the name for God in Arabic. The following verse from the Quran (112) indicates the identity of God in the Islamic sense:

**Say He is God—the One.**
**Beyond eternity, never begun.**
**No father has He, nor son.**
**There is none like Him, not one.**

This verse is considered so important that Muhammad described it as equivalent to one third of the entire Quran.

After receiving the first five lines of the Quran, Muhammad was shaken by the weight of the revelation, both physically and spiritually. He fled the cave and entered his home quaking. "Cover me! Cover me!" he cried to his wife Khadijah, who wrapped him in blankets and embraced him. Muhammad thought that he had gone insane or had been possessed by a *jinn* (a nonhuman spirit). But his calm and intelligent wife was firmly convinced of his mental stability and excellent character. He was known throughout Mecca as al-Amin (the trustworthy). Khadijah consoled Muhammad that what he had experienced in the cave could only have been real and true.

With the revelation of the first verses of the Quran to Muhammad, the Islamic faith was born. Khadijah was the first person to accept the message of Muhammad and by the end of Muhammad's life, the Muslim community numbered around 30,000. Today there are more than one billion Muslims worldwide.

## what is islam?

Being a Muslim includes two basic beliefs: Belief in one God (Allah), and belief that Muhammad is a messenger and prophet of God. A person who believes this second component must necessarily believe in two additional things: Muhammad's message, the Quran, which is

The Quran, the Muslim holy book, as revealed to Muhammad. He recited each verse as he received it, determining its specific location in the Quran in relation to the other verses revealed to him. Muhammad instructed scribes to record the text, and they did so initially on any suitable object and surface, using the leaves of trees; pieces of wood, parchment, and leather; flat stones; and shoulder blades.

seen as the literal word of God; and Muhammad's example, called his *sunnah*, which was recorded in detail by those close to him and has been preserved over time.

The Quran, then, is the textbook of spiritual and practical guidelines by which a Muslim lives his or her life, and the *sunnah* of Muhammad is an unfolding illustration, a series of real-life examples, of the ideas contained in the Quran.

One of the best ways to approach the Quran is to recite it, because it is essentially a recitation. The person reciting the Quran becomes like a hollow earthen vessel echoing the resonance of the Quran. This inner resonance connects the person to God. But understanding the meaning is equally important. Muslims say that God speaks to people through the Quran, and people speak to God through prayer and supplication.

Islam is a religion of action and pertains to every aspect of life, from the mundane (eating, drinking, sleeping, waking, working, studying, even going to the bathroom) to the spiritual (praying, fasting, meditating). Muhammad once said, "The best Islam is that you feed the hungry and spread peace among people you know and those you do not know."

Muslims are required to perform five key acts of worship: testifying that there is no god but God, praying five times a day, fasting during the Islamic month of Ramadan, giving a certain percentage of their income each year to the needy, and performing the pilgrimage to Mecca once in a lifetime.

All Islamic acts of worship have one goal: to become increasingly conscious of the existence of God: "Oh you who have attained to faith! Remain conscious of God, and seek to come closer to Him, and strive hard in his cause, so that you might attain to a happy state." (Quran 5:35)

For a Muslim, striving to live according to God's way is simultaneously a cause and an effect of a heightened spiritual awareness. The greater one's awareness of God's presence, the more one desires to live according to the guidelines set down by him; and the more one lives according to God's guidelines, the closer one feels to him. Attaining a happy state—one imbued with a divine awareness—refers to happiness in this life and happiness in the one to come, the afterlife.

After the Quran was revealed to Muhammad, he reviewed it with the angel Gabriel once a year, and twice in the last year of his life. Muslims believe that the Quran has not been changed since it was revealed to Muhammad and take heart in the statement: "Behold, it is we ourselves who have bestowed from on high, step by step, this Quran and, behold, it is we who shall truly guard it (from all corruption)." (Quran 15:9)

Islam seeks to answer the deepest questions of human identity: who are we, where did we come from, why are we here, and where are we going? The answers necessitate a journey of self-discovery, and, eventually, a surrender of the self. Ultimately, a Muslim is a person who is willing to journey, to investigate, and to face the anguish and exhilaration that come with deep self-inquiry.

## The quest of the spiritual wayfarer

Islamic theology states that human beings are created of an earthly entity and a spiritual entity. The spiritual is said to be universal while the earthly is localized. In other words, the spiritual is not bound by the limitations of earthly domains and contains universal abilities. This is why Muslims believe that, with God's grace, the sheer potential of any one human being is limitless.

Further, the spiritual realm is everlasting and eternal while the earthly realm is fleeting and temporal. This leads to a concept that is central to Islam, the belief that the world is a land of illusions and that everything in it will fade away. Nothing is meant to stay the same, and nothing is meant to last. Death and dissolution are crafted into the very fabric of earthly existence. The Quran says, "Whatever you are given here is but the enjoyment of this life: but that which is with God is better and more lasting; it is for those who believe and put their trust in their Lord." (Quran 42:36)

Islam holds that whatever a person does, life should ultimately be devoted to a search for its essence, the deeper reality. In other words, whether a person chooses to be a philosopher, a scientist, or a rock star, one's vocation is simply the outward expression of an inner search. The human being is considered a microcosm of the universe, according to Islamic theologians, so the traveler must journey through the outer, earthly realm as well as the inner, spiritual realm. Within each realm, there are signs pointing the way. "In the creation of the earth and the unfolding of night and day are signs for those of understanding." (Quran 3:190)

Sustaining both the earthly and the spiritual realms is the realm of the One. Everything has a natural tendency to flow toward the One. Once the self realizes the need to rise toward the One, it desires to join with the flow and surrenders to it. This surrender is called Islam.

Interfering with the flow is like blocking a river in its natural path to the ocean, causing a disturbance in the river. It is also compared to keeping apart two people in love, an act that can only result in confusion and grief. In the same way, if the spiritual self is prevented from flowing toward God, the whole realm becomes filled with grief.

Muslims have a special relationship with their prophet, who the Quran says is "closer to the believers than they are to themselves." (33:6) In moving through life, Muslims look for leadership in the *sunnah* of Muhammad because he has already traveled the best route and his journey is documented. Through knowing him and emulating his way, a person finds what is known as the Straight Path, which leads to the core of the spiritual self, known as the self-at-peace.

So the answer to the Muslim seeker's question "Who am I?" may be that humans are spiritual beings clothed in veils of flesh and blood; when the flesh and blood pass away, the true being emerges; that this earthly life exists only as the reflection of a higher life; that feelings, desires and passions, and love and intimacy are only reflections of deeper, more intense emotions arising from another spiritual place; and that a person's true identity originates beyond this world.

# one

# ORIGINS

## The man and His message

Muhammad, the prophet of Islam, lived 1,400 years ago in the desert of Arabia. Over the twenty-two years of his mission, from the time of the revelation until his death, he explained the fundamentals of the Islamic religion, as revealed to him by God, and illustrated them in the society he set up in Medina (known as the City of Light).

The spiritual matrix of the religion was revealed during the first twelve years of Muhammad's mission when he was in Mecca. After fleeing persecution, Muhammad spent the next ten years in Medina solidifying the social structure of the Muslim *ummah* or community. By the time Muhammad died at age sixty-five, the fundamentals of Islam were set in place, and, to this day, are observed by Muslims the world over.

Muhammad lived in a culture and era different from the Western world of today. Yet Muslims believe he was chosen by God to deliver a universal message to humanity—for all peoples, of all cultures, at all times. Heeding the Quranic verses revealed to him, Muhammad separated himself from many of the cultural habits and practices of his day and set an example for others to follow. He freed slaves and encouraged others to do the same at a time when slavery was commonplace. He banned female infanticide at a time when girl babies were sometimes buried in the sand. He limited the number of wives a man could have when huge harems among the wealthy were the order of the day. He gave women set shares in inheritance at a time when they regularly received nothing. He taught the equality of human beings by counting rich and poor, black and white, male and female among his closest companions. He taught humility by living humbly, without material trappings, by washing his own dishes, and by acting on the council of others, including that of his wives. He taught graciousness by treating people, creatures, and the earth with dignity and compassion and exercised forbearance and forgiveness by pardoning even those most vehemently against him.

The life story of Muhammad is called the *sira*. The detailed accounts of his sayings and actions are called the *hadith*. Together, the *sira* and the *hadith* make up the *sunnah* and illustrate the principles laid down in the Quran. The Quran and the *sunnah* form the bedrock of the Islamic religion. Modern Islamic law (*shariah*) is based on the Quran and on extrapolations from the actions of Muhammad. Muslims from around the world study Muhammad's biography and strive to apply it to their own modern lives.

## The mecca years

The pre-Islamic Arabs were fierce in upholding a human ideal (*muruwwah*), which included traits such as generosity, courage, honesty, justice, equality, concern for the needs of the poor and weak, patience in suffering, and avenging wrongdoings.

The Arabs worshipped a number of gods, including three female goddesses, in the form of idols that they housed in the Ka'bah. Foreign traders and pilgrims brought their own idols with them when they came to Mecca, and these gods too were installed in the Ka'bah. Muhammad's family, the Banu Hashim, a branch of the Quraysh tribe and one of the most important families in the region, became the esteemed caretakers of the holy Ka'bah.

It was into this context that Muhamamd was born in about 570. His father died before he was born and his mother died when he was six, leaving Muhammad orphaned.

It was the custom of well-to-do families to send their children to live with Bedouin families in the desert to learn the pure Arabic language. Muhammad ended up with a foster mother called Halima who noted that prosperity came to her household after the arrival of Muhammad. He was known to wander off into the desert, and Halima reported that he loved to be outside under the starry night sky. Once Muhammad disappeared for some time and Halima went out in search of him. She was worried that he was lost in the desert when a voice said to her, "Do not worry—he is not lost to you! Someday the whole world will be lost in him!"

Muhammad was later taken into the care of his uncle Abu Talib. His uncle was not a wealthy man, so Muhammad tended sheep and goats to earn extra money, spending hours alone in the desert. As a result, he never learned to read or write. When Muhammad became a little older, his uncle, a trader, took him on caravan expeditions.

On one such trip to Syria, the caravan halted beneath a tree to rest during the hottest hours of the day. Abu Talib and Muhammad happened to stop near the cave of a monk who lived a life of solitary retreat. The monk had studied ancient religious manuscripts that spoke of the coming of a prophet to the Arabs. When the monk saw the caravan approaching from the south, he wondered if that spiritual person was among the travelers. The curious monk invited the people of the caravan to eat with him, insisting that they bring every member of the group. Abu Talib gathered everyone together, and they sat down with the monk. Scanning their faces, the monk sensed that no special spiritual presence was among them, so he said, "Is this your whole group? Don't leave anyone behind, bring everyone to eat with us."

Muhammad was brought over to eat, and the monk realized that the boy had a spirituality about him. The monk then asked Muhammad a series of questions, which Muhammad readily answered. Muhammad even lifted up his shirt when the monk asked to see his back. The monk was sure that this must be the prophet of the Arabs, and the mark on Muhammad's back confirmed it. There, between the boy's shoulder blades, was a raised mark, the seal of prophethood Gabriel had placed there after he opened Muhammad's chest and washed his heart in a bowl of Zamzam water, removing malice and filling him with gentleness, knowledge, faith, certitude, and submission. As the caravan was preparing to leave, the monk said to Abu Talib, "Take this boy back to his country and guard him. Great things are in store for this boy of yours."

## muhammad's household

By the time Muhammad reached the age of twenty-five, he had developed a reputation of being honest, just, and of sound character. People would leave their valuables with him for safekeeping. A wealthy, widowed businesswoman named Khadijah, asked the highly esteemed young man to take her goods to Syria to sell. Muhammad agreed and undertook her trading mission with much success. Khadijah was so impressed with Muhammad's character that she proposed marriage, despite their age difference—Khadijah was forty.

Muhammad and Khadijah lived a happy life, surrounded by a large family. Together they had four girls and two boys (who died in infancy). Muhammad also took over the care of Abu Talib's son Ali and adopted a former slave called Zayd.

The story of Zayd's adoption reveals the situation of slaves in the time of Muhammad and how the Prophet himself dealt with it. In the early days of Islam, slaves were often Africans from across the Red Sea. But as the Islamic influence spread, slaves were taken from among the peoples of North Africa, central Asia, parts of Europe, and the Caucacus. Although the Quran did not outright abolish slavery, a widespread institution at the time, it laid down legal and moral guidelines for the treatment of slaves. Muslims could not enslave other Muslims, but a slave could become Muslim. A Muslim slave had the same spiritual merit as a free Muslim did. The freeing of a slave was encouraged as an act of charity, and all slaves were to be treated with kindness. If a slave woman gave birth to her master's child, the child was born free and the master was responsible for the woman and the child thereafter. Slaves could own land, lead Friday prayers, and hold certain offices. There are periods in Islamic history when freed slaves, known as Mamluks, held positions of great power. In parts of Syria and Egypt, Mamluks ruled for centuries.

## The first Believers

In his fortieth year, when Muhammad received the first lines of the Quran in the cave of Hira he was descending the mountain when he heard a voice say, "You are the messenger of God and I am Gabriel." Muhammad looked up and saw Gabriel in his angelic form. Again the voice said, "You are the messenger of God and I am Gabriel." In every direction he looked, all Muhammad could see was the angel encompassing the entire horizon.

Khadijah was the first person who Muhammad instructed in the ritual ablution and prayers taught to him by Gabriel. The next people he taught were his cousin Ali, at that time about ten years old; his adopted son, Zayd; and his close childhood friend Abu Bakr. Abu Bakr was widely respected in Mecca, and many people came to Islam through him. Others came through mystical routes, summonded by dreams or visions or voices heard in the desert.

The little group of Muslims practiced their faith in private during these early days, fearing the rejection of the community. But they were passionate about their new religion and meticulous about performing their ablutions, keeping their clothes and bodies clean, praying on time, and correctly and perfectly memorizing the verses of the Quran that continued to be revealed to Muhammad. These early verses were short and expressed spiritual perspectives on existence. They emphasized the ephemeral nature of the material world, the certainty of the afterlife, the existence of heaven and hell and, overall, the importance of recognizing one God and his messengers, including Muhammad.

## They Know Not What They Do

Islam began to spread quietly and peacefully among the population. After about three years, Muhammad was commanded to proclaim the message publicly when he received this verse: "Warn (whomever you can reach, beginning with) your kinsfolk, and spread the wings of your tenderness over all of the believers who may follow you." (Quran 26:214–215)

The time had come for Muhammad to actively spread his message. His first step was to invite his entire clan to dinner. After the meal, Muhammad said to them, "I know of no Arab who has come to his people with a nobler message than mine. I bring you the best of this world and the next. God has commanded me to call you to him. Which of you, then, will help me in this?" There was silence in the room. Finally, Ali spoke up and offered his support. The men rose to their feet, laughing at the pledge of a thirteen-year-old boy, and left the room. Little did they know the shape of Ali's future: he grew up as one of Muhammad's closest companions and eventually became the fourth caliph, or leader, of the Muslim *ummah*.

Islam's message of humility and equality appealed to less privileged members of society, while others felt threatened by it. They saw the new religion as disrespecting the traditions of their forefathers and rejecting their gods and idols. They disliked Muhammad's message as well because it interfered with their economy, which was based on pilgrimage to the idols of the Ka'bah.

At first, they tried to dissuade Muhammad peacefully, offering him money, women, and leadership of the community if only he would give up his mission. He responded by saying, "If you placed the sun in my right hand and the moon in my left hand on the condition that

I abandon this course before he has made it victorious, or I have perished, I would not abandon my message."

Over time, it became increasingly clear that Muhammad himself had little influence over who accepted his message and who did not. Some of his closest relatives were the most hostile toward him, and even his beloved uncle Abu Talib never accepted Islam. Muhammad's lack of influence is reflected in the Quranic phrase addressed to him: "You cannot guide aright everyone whom you love, but it is God who guides whomever he wills." (Quran 28:56)

There is a well-known story about an enemy of Muhammad, known for his hatred of Islam. Thumama, who was the leader of a powerful tribe and had taken the lives of many of Muhammad's followers, vowing to kill as many more as he could find, including Muhammad. One day, some of Muhammad's followers captured Thumama in the desert and brought him to Muhammad. Upon seeing Thumama tied to a pole, Muhammad asked that the prisoner be freed and placed instead in the room Muhammad reserved for his guests. He then requested that a meal be prepared for the man. After Thumama finished his meal, Muhammad went to him and said, "What do you have to say for yourself?" to which Thumama replied, "Either set me free or kill me that I may die with my honor." Muhammad returned the next day and had the same conversation with Thumama, and the day after that. On the third day, Muhammad asked that Thumama be set free, much to the astonishment of his companions. Thumama retreated into the desert.

But he had not gone far when he stopped at a grove of palms and washed himself. Then Muhammad's companions saw a figure walking back toward them. To their amazement, it was Thumama saying in a clear voice, "I bear witness that there is no god but God and I bear witness that Muhammad is his servant and his messenger." Then he went to Muhammad, and said, "Until today there was no face on earth that I hated more than yours; now there is no face on earth that I love more than yours." Thumama's transformation proved critical. Through his sincere and influential leadership, Thumama had a great effect on the establishment and spread of Islam.

Despite Thumama's conversion, the abuse and hostility toward Muhammad increased; people slandered him and threw stones and garbage at him. Sometimes violence was used against him and his followers—but God had not given the Muslims permission to use violence in return, and Muhammad encouraged his small community to be patient. He would pray for those who were against him saying, "God, guide them on the right path for they know not what they do."

Eventually, the persecution reached a point where emigration would be preferable to the suffering they were enduring. Muhammad knew that the land of Abyssinia, in modern-day Ethiopia, was ruled by a pious Christian king, and Muhammad encouraged many of his followers to go there until the harassment decreased. About eighty Muslims embarked on the first emigration in Islam, fleeing to Abyssinia where they were well received and allowed to practice freely.

## muhammad's night journey

After the immigration to Abyssinia, another major turning point occurred—called *al-isra* or the Night Journey. According to Islamic tradition, late one night, when Muhammad was at the Ka'bah, the angel Gabriel approached him and led him outside to a white-winged, horselike beast. Muhammad mounted the steed, and it took flight with Gabriel keeping pace beside them. The three of them flew northward and landed in Jerusalem, an incident that is mentioned in the Quran: "Limitless is he in his glory who transported his servant by night from the Mosque of the Sanctuary (at Mecca) to the Far Mosque (at Jerusalem) . . . so that we might show him some of our symbols." (Quran 17:1)

In Jerusalem at the site now known as the Dome of the Rock, Muhammad met all the past prophets. Then, after Muhammad prayed, he mounted the white steed and they ascended through the seven heavens, a journey called *al-miraj* or ascension. Along the way, Muhammad caught glimpses of the prophets again. He later reported on the beauty of the inhabitants he saw in paradise—particularly that of the prophets Joseph and Aaron.

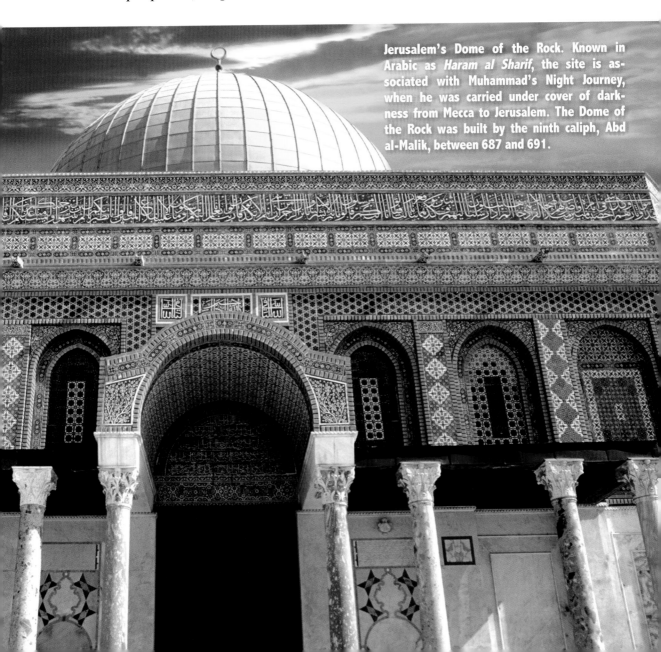

Jerusalem's Dome of the Rock. Known in Arabic as *Haram al Sharif*, the site is associated with Muhammad's Night Journey, when he was carried under cover of darkness from Mecca to Jerusalem. The Dome of the Rock was built by the ninth caliph, Abd al-Malik, between 687 and 691.

Muhammad's journey went as far as the Lote Tree, described in the Quran as the point where knowledge ends, beyond which no human or angel can proceed. There, beyond the branches of the Lote Tree, God revealed himself to Muhammad, an event mentioned in the Quran: "Truly did he see some of the most profound of his Sustainer's symbols." (Quran 53:18). It was there that Muhammad received the command that Muslims should pray five times a day. The angel then escorted Muhammad to Jerusalem, then back to Mecca. It was still night when he returned. His journey had taken place in the twinkling of an eye.

When Muhammad's enemies heard of his experience, they were overjoyed. Every child of the desert knew that it took more than a month to go from Mecca to Jerusalem by camel and the same amount of time to come back. Now Muhammad was claiming that he had made the journey in one night? His enemies had called Muhammad many names; now they could add "liar" to the litany.

## The Medina Years

Shortly before Muhammad's Night Journey, he lost two supporters in one year: his beloved wife Khadijah and his uncle and protector Abu Talib. As tensions between the Quraysh and the Muslims increased, Muhammad went to the nearby mountain town of Taif to see if the people there would embrace the message of Islam. But he was rejected in Taif.

At the same time, some two hundred miles north of Mecca, in the oasis town of Yathrib, tribal tensions were rife. The people living there, a mixture of pagan Arabs and monotheistic Jews, were looking for someone who could possibly unite their fractured land. Some of the people of Yathrib had encountered Muhammad during the annual pilgrimage to Mecca and had embraced Islam. They wondered if Muhammad might be the man to bring peace to their city.

## Hijrah

In 622 a delegation of men from Yathrib came to Mecca and pledged themselves to Muhammad. The terms of the agreement were unequivocal: the tribes of Yathrib and the community of Muslims from Mecca would mutually support each other under the leadership of Muhammad. After the pledge was sealed, Muslims began to emigrate from Mecca to Yathrib and the once lively and prospering town of Mecca took on a feeling of emptiness. The Quraysh watched the flow of people out of their city with dismay and decided that something must be done to prevent it. They agreed to assign one young, able-bodied man from each clan to deal Muhammad a mortal blow—thus his blood would be on all of their hands.

As they were plotting his murder, Muhammad went to Abu Bakr and told him to prepare to emigrate. He then returned to his house and gave Ali his cloak telling him to lie in his bed. Muhammad began to recite a verse of the Quran describing the nonbelievers and when he came to the words "and we have enshrouded them in veils so that they cannot see,"(36:9) he slipped out of the house. When the young men looked into Muhammad's room they saw a body covered in a cloak on the bed and were confident that Muhammad was inside. But as dawn was breaking and a man on the street claimed to have seen Muhammad elsewhere, a search party set out to find him.

Meanwhile, Muhammad and Abu Bakr had mounted their camels and were heading for the cavernous mountains to the south of Mecca. As the oasis town of Yathrib lay to the north, their plan was to hide in a cave to the south to avoid capture. They hid in a cave for three days, while search parties went out in all directions from Mecca. At one point, a search party approached the cave. Muhammad whispered to his companion, "Grieve not: God is with us." (Quran 9:40)

Muhammad and Abu Bakr then started on their journey to Yathrib and arrived twelve days later in the town of Quba on the fringes of the oasis, where Muhammad laid the foundations of Islam's first *masjid* (mosque). The word *masjid* means "a place of prostrations" and in pre-Islamic times the area around the Ka'bah was called the *masjid*. Now the Muslims had their own mosque.

They continued into Yathrib where they received a warm welcome. People pulled on the reins of Muhammad's camel, asking him to stop and settle with them. But Muhammad kept going, keeping a loose hold on the reins, saying, "Let her go her way for she is under the command of God."

Eventually the camel stopped and knelt on a piece of ground. Taking this as a sign, Muhammad purchased the land and built another mosque there with adjoining houses for himself and his family. Yathrib became known after the arrival of Muhammad as "al-Medina al-Nabi" (the City of the Prophet) or more simply, Medina.

This emigration to Medina, after twelve years of persecution in Mecca, is known as the *hijrah*. It was a momentous event in Islamic history because the Muslim community was now free to practice its new religion in peace and, under the guidance of Muhammad, sculpt a society based on the words of the Quran. The community that had matured under the stress of persecution was now ready to assume the dynamic role envisaged for it in the Quran with Muhammad as its leader. The year of the hijrah, 622 C.E., became the first year of the Islamic calendar.

## city of the prophet

Islam was now established in Medina, and Muhammad set about building a community based on the Islamic faith. The Muslims who fled Mecca with Muhammad became known as the "emigrants," and those in Medina who became Muslims and supported Muhammad became known as the "helpers." Initially, each emigrant was paired with a helper to smooth the integration of the two groups.

## Travel someplace better...

The word *hijrah* denotes the migration of a person or social group from one physical environment to another, a relocation motivated by the hope of reaching an environment more conducive to the moral and material well-being of that person or group. Some modern Muslims consider the *hijrah* an ongoing possibility or option framing their lives. They believe that if they migrate to a place having conditions more conducive to living a righteous life, they will eventually be rewarded in heaven, as promised in the Quran: "... If anyone leaves his home, fleeing from evil unto God and his Messenger, and then death overtakes him—his reward is ready with God ..." (4:100)

There was also a third group living in the oasis town: several Jewish tribes. Jewish writings foretold of the coming of a prophet, and many followers were awaiting his arrival. When they learned that an Arab was claiming to be a prophet, it was difficult for them to believe that God would send a prophet who was not a Jew. Still, most were curious about this man from Mecca. Muhammad hoped that he would be accepted by the Jewish tribes and be able to unify the two faiths.

These Jewish tribes had good reason to support Muhammad because he was the most powerful man in the region. He had united the warring Arab tribes and drafted what is considered to be one of the first written constitutions, the Constitution of Medina *(Dustur al-Medina),* guaranteeing the basic human rights of freedom of faith and security of every individual regardless of race or religion. This constitution, written in 622, also pledged mutual support against any outside enemy hostile to the people of the oasis. Thus Muhammad aimed to create a unified community while leaving room for the differences between the faiths. Jews, Muslims, and pagans alike signed the Medina Constitution. Although Muhammad never pressed the

Jews to accept his prophecy, he was referred to in the constitution as the "Messenger of God." The Jews agreed that all matters of conflict would be referred to him.

Two other important developments occurred shortly after Muhammad's arrival in Medina. He received a revelation to pray facing Mecca rather than facing Jerusalem, as the Muslims had done previously. This event held a deep significance for Muslims and helped to centralize the Islamic faith. In addition, Muhammad established the method of calling people to prayer five times a day.

## The First Raids

Up to this point, the followers of Muhammad had not used physical resistance against those who persecuted them. But once in Medina, a revelation came to Muhammad giving Muslims permission to fight.

The community in Medina turned its thoughts to the idea of raids. Raiding caravans had been a means of livelihood for the tribes of Arabia. As the tribes were often at war with one another, raiding caravans proved a means of surviving the often stark conditions that prevailed in the arid peninsula. Since the Muslims had left their homes quickly and under duress, they had little to survive on. The justification for the raids was not only historical but also based on the idea that by raiding a caravan coming or going to Mecca, the Muslims would be reclaiming the value of the possessions they had left behind. Medina lay on the trade route between Mecca and Damascus. Word came to Muhammad in 624 that a well-stocked caravan was returning to Mecca from Syria by way of Medina, and he readied his people to intercept it.

But the caravan leaders heard of the Muslims' plans and sent word of their own to Mecca. In Mecca, a large army was quickly assembled and set out to intercept the small band of Muslims. The two groups met on the plain of Badr near the coast of the Red Sea.

**Indian Muslims face the direction of Mecca while praying on the last Friday of the Islamic holy month of Ramadan. The five-times-daily call to prayer is one of the Five Pillars and a cornerstone of the faith.**

The caravan managed to slip by and reach the safety of Mecca, and the two unequal armies were left to face each other. Three hundred Muslims were pitted against a thousand Meccans.

An incident that happened just before the two armies fought illustrates a key point regarding the character of Muhammad. He was known to listen to the advice of others when it came to matters of which he possessed little or no knowledge. In this case, Muhammad ordered his men to halt at the first well they came to, but one of his companions queried his instructions, asking him whether it was a decision made by divine decree. Muhammad answered that it was by his own reckoning, whereby the man laid out a better plan: to continue until they had the majority of the wells under their control thus depriving the enemy of water. This proved to be a successful strategy, and the Muslims took on the Meccans in the first war of Islam, known as the battle of Badr. The Muslims won a decisive victory, and the retreating Meccans vowed to avenge themselves in the coming year.

The Quran contains references to the concept of war in Islam. Violence is sanctioned in cases of self-defense: "Permission to fight is given to those against whom war is being wrongfully waged—and, verily, God has indeed the power to help them—and to those who have been driven from their homelands against all right for no other reason than their saying, 'Our Sustainer is God!' The verse continues: "For if God had not enabled people to defend themselves against one another, all monasteries and churches and synagogues and mosques— in all of which God's name is abundantly extolled—would surely have been destroyed." (Quran 22:39–40)

Thus the Quran states that self-defense can morally justify a war. Muslims are obligated to defend not only their own political and religious freedom but also the freedom of people of other faiths living peacefully among them. Muhammad also forbade the Muslims from destroying dwellings, crops, and trees. Women, children, and animals (except those animals ridden into warfare) are also protected.

Another important reference to war is found in this verse: "And fight in God's cause against those who wage war against you, but do not yourselves commit aggression—for God does not love the aggressors." (Quran 2:190) This verse commands Muslims to fight only according to the ethical principles ordained by God—in self-defense and to avoid aggression.

The Quran notes the importance of knowledge and education— intellectual as well as physical striving—for the development of a community even during wartime: ". . . it is not desirable that all of the believers take the field [in time of war]. From within every group in their midst, some shall refrain from going forth to war, and shall devote themselves [instead] to acquiring a deeper knowledge of the faith, and teach their homecoming brethren, so that these too might guard themselves against evil." (Quran 9:122)

## character

Every prophet has a specific character. Muhammad himself was a multitalented individual. He was a prophet, a head of state, a community leader, and a warrior. He was a mediator of disputes, a judge on matters large and small, and a revolutionary social reformer. He was also a loving husband, father, and friend. Along with his various responsibilities, Muhammad milked his goat, mended his clothes, repaired his shoes, washed his dishes, helped with household work, visited the sick, joined the games of children as he passed by, and interacted lovingly with his wives.

Muhammad, through his actions and character, embodied the ideals of *murawwah*. The essence of Muhammad's mission lay in mercy. He is named in the Quran as "a mercy to all the worlds" (7:158; 21:107) because his character and the nature of his message appeal to humanity, irrespective of race or culture.

Mercy, in reference to Muhammad, includes a spectrum of inner qualities such as love, compassion, kindness, forgiveness, beauty, understanding, clemency, gentleness, grace, and subtlety. There is no end to the lyrical descriptions of poetry praising Muhammad's qualities. An Urdu poet says of him: "Beauty from head to toe, love embodied."

Muhammad extended his loving kindness to all beings. He had a particular love of children. On one occasion, he prayed with an infant in his arms, placing the little one on the ground when he went into *sujud* (prostration). Muhammad was also known for his love of animals, especially cats. Islamic scholar and author Annemarie Schimmel asks, "Did he not cut the sleeve from his coat when he had to get up for his prayer and yet did not want to disturb the cat that was sleeping on the sleeve? One of his cats even gave birth to kittens on his coat."

Muhammad respected women in his own good treatment of his wives and served as a model for the men of his community. He emphasized the equality of men and women in terms of their religious obligations: the major ones (praying, fasting, paying *zakat*, and performing the pilgrimage) as well as the more subtle ones, such as striving to treat people well. The Quran gave women rights in the areas of inheritance, marriage, divorce, and fair treatment. In Islam, a woman is encouraged to select a good husband and has the right to initiate a divorce in certain cases. Although a woman usually inherits less than what her male relatives do, men are financially responsible for their families whereas women are not. Muhammad emphasized respect due to the mother, saying that paradise lies at her feet. He identified four women as the noblest in human history. They are Asiya, wife of one of the pharaohs; Mary, mother of Jesus; Khadijah, the first wife of Muhammad; and Fatima, Muhammad's daughter. Each woman had unique attributes that Muslim women today strive to attain.

In accordance with the traditions of the time, Muhammad had more than one wife. But apart from young Aishah, the daughter of Abu Bakr, most of his wives were widowed women. As Muslim men were killed in battle, often women and children were left in need of care. There were other reasons for polygamy during Muhammad's time. It was practical in terms of aiding survival in the harsh social and physical environment. In pre-Islamic times, men who could afford to had large harems of wives, but the Quran limited the number of wives a man could take to four and established criteria that made it difficult for a man to take even that number.

Among Muhammad's wives were a Jewish woman called Safiyah and a Christian woman named Maria, both of whom adopted Islam. One *hadith* relates that Muhammad once found Safiyah crying because another of his wives had insulted her. Muhammad said: "You are the daughter of the prophet Aaron, your uncle was the prophet Moses, and you are the wife of the prophet Muhammad, so why should anyone be scornful toward you?"

The life of Muhammad was a humble one—and seemed to get humbler as his mission progressed. As his wife Aishah recounted, "We would sight three new moons without lighting a fire to cook a meal in the Prophet's houses." They were sustained by dates, water, and camel milk given to them by neighbors. A *hadith* says: "He was well acquainted with sorrow, much absorbed in thought, had little rest, was silent for long periods, did not talk without cause, and never found blame in anything."

## Breaches and Battles

After the battle of Badr, some Jews began claiming that they were not bound by the terms of the Medina Constitution. They were worried about the increasing influence of Muhammad, and one of the tribes started communicating with his enemies in Mecca. This tribe thus disregarded the covenant and as a consequence it was exiled from the oasis. The members settled north of Medina, and some went as far as the borders of Syria. This was the first Jewish tribe to be exiled from Medina, according to Muslim accounts.

In the following years, two other significant battles took place between the Meccans and the Muslims of Medina. The first was the battle of Uhud, in 625, when a huge Meccan army defeated the Muslims. As revenge for the losses they suffered in Badr, the Meccans even mutilated the bodies of some of the dead Muslims. In 627, after much planning, the Meccans descended on Medina only to find the city defended by a trench dug around it. In this, the battle of the

Trench, the Meccans tried for thirty days to cross the trench but did not succeed and returned to Mecca.

## peace on the plain

Certain months of the year had been considered holy since pre-Islamic times, and their sanctity was confirmed in the Quran. One of them, Ramadan, the ninth month of the lunar calendar, was the month when the hajj or pilgrimage to Mecca was undertaken. Six years after leaving Mecca, in 628, Muhammad decided it was time to embark on the annual journey. His intention was to dress in the white garb of a pilgrim and enter Mecca without weapons, in a ritually pure state. At first his followers were shocked by the idea—walk into enemy territory totally defenseless? But Muhammad held firm, and 1,400 people decided to join him.

As the group traveled south, the Meccans got news that the pilgrims were approaching. They were unsure how to react. On one hand, how could they, the honorable hosts of the holy house, turn away a group of pilgrims on whom their reputation and livelihood were based? On the other hand, this particular group of pilgrims was their enemy.

When the Muslims reached the plain of Hudaybiyah on the outskirts of Mecca, a delegation of Meccans went out to meet them to try to avert the pilgrims. After intense negotiations, Muhammad reached an agreement with the Meccans: the groundbreaking Treaty of Hudaybiyah, which stipulated peace between the two groups.

## the siege of mecca

This peace lasted for almost a year, and again the season for pilgrimage was approaching when, a man from Mecca killed one of the Muslims. Muhammad considered this a breach of the Treaty of Hudaybiyah. At the head of ten thousand Muslims, Muhammad rode into Mecca.

According to accounts, his head was bowed low over his camel, touching the animal's back, in humility to God. Many of the Meccans fled to the hills above the town to watch the Muslims enter the city. But when the Meccans realized that Muhammad and his people would bring peace to the city, almost everyone eventually surrendered to the Muslims. The Muslims had peacefully seized Mecca.

Muhammad was now the leader of most of the Arabian Peninsula. His following had grown; he was victorious in battle. People in Mecca and in Arabia had been waiting to see which side would emerge victorious, Muhammad or the pagans. Many believed that victory for Muhammad would mean that he was a genuine prophet. When Muhammad indeed emerged as the victor, they approached him with enthusiasm. Muhammad granted amnesty to each person in Mecca who agreed to follow the path of Islam.

## Muhammad's Final Year

Every year, Muhammad spent the last ten days of the holy month of Ramadan in spiritual retreat in the mosque in Medina. During this period, the angel Gabriel came to recite the entire Quran with him to make sure that none of it had slipped from his memory. But in the final year of his life, Muhammad and Gabriel recited the Quran twice.

That year, 632, Muhammad led the pilgrimage to Mecca with more than 70,000 people, setting the final example for others to follow. According to Muslim tradition, Abraham had ordained aspects of the pilgrimage that the Arabs of Mecca had over time dropped or changed. Muhammad corrected the pilgrimage rite, and people to this day perform it as he did in 632.

At one point in the pilgrimage, on the plain of Arafat within the vicinity of Mecca, Muhammad preached what was to be his last sermon. He finished with the question: "Oh people, have I faithfully delivered unto

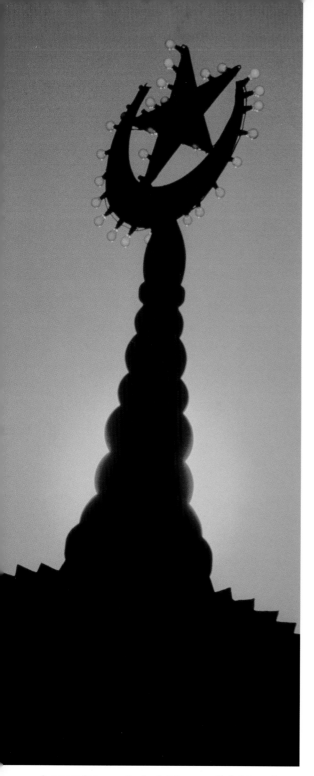

**A towering symbol of Islam: a finial bearing the characteristic crescent and star icon.**

you my message?" A powerful rumble of assent issued from the throats of the Muslims assembled before him, "Yes!" Muhammad raised his forefinger and said, "Oh God, bear witness!"

## Death of the prophet

Shortly after the pilgrimage, Muhammad developed a headache and a fever that did not subdue. He continued to lead the prayers until one day he addressed his people saying, "There is a slave among the slaves of God unto whom God has offered the choice between this world and that which is with him. And the slave has chosen that which is with God."

When his companion Abu Bakr heard this, he began to cry because he knew that Muhammad was speaking of himself and that his death was near. As Muhammad's illness progressed, he led the prayers while seated, his congregation seated also, until one day even this became impossible for him. For the first time, someone other than Muhammad was to lead the community in prayer. Muhammad assigned the task to Abu Bakr, while the ailing Prophet spent most of his time in Aishah's room, lying with his head on her lap. One day his head grew heavier and heavier until Aishah realized that he was dead.

Hearing the news of Muhammad's death, the community reeled from shock and grief; confusion reigned and some of his closest companions refused to believe it. But Abu Bakr had seen Muhammad's body himself. He went immediately to the mosque and addressed the crowd:

"Oh people! Whoever worshiped Muhammad, be informed that Muhammad is dead. But whosoever worshiped God, be informed that God is alive and never dies."

Then he recited a verse from the Quran: "Muhammad is only a messenger, and all the other messengers have passed away before him. If, then, he dies or be slain, will you then turn upon your heels?" (3:144) With these words, Abu Bakr reminded the community to worship God rather than worshipping Muhammad.

The Muslims were not aggrieved for Muhammad because they knew, as he had taught them, that death was the ultimate meeting with God. But they were saddened for themselves and the loss of Muhammad's light and guidance in their own community. To this day, the Islamic *ummah* looks on the life of Muhammad as the brightest days of its history.

# two

# EVOLUTION

## Rise of an Empire

Over the course of twenty-two years, Muhammad established the foundations of the Islamic civilization. By the time of his death, in 632, Islam had spread to much of the Arabian Peninsula and within a few centuries it had spread throughout western Asia and North Africa. As Muslims emerged from the Arabian Peninsula, they absorbed customs, influenced cultures, gained knowledge, and spread the message of Islam across a vast geographical range.

Modern Muslims feel close to their history. Despite a 1,400-year gap, they love Muhammad as they love their living friends and relatives. They examine his life story, strive to emulate him in all manner of daily life, and study the personalities and histories of his closest companions and wives. Islamic jurists make judgments based on Muhammad's *sunnah*. Some sects mourn the deaths of Muhammad's grandsons with elaborate rituals, and Muslim students the world over learn the classical Arabic of the Quran.

## The First Caliph

By the end of his life, Muhammad had united war-torn Arabia and had pacified the fractious tribes. But Muhammad never formally assigned a successor. The question that arose after his death was, Who will lead the Islamic community?

In the confusion following Muhammad's death, it was Muhammad's companion Umar who prompted a solution. According to the accounts of Muhammad's life story, as his body was being washed in preparation for burial, Umar addressed a group of people who were debating where the community's authority should lie.

"Do you not remember that the Messenger of God ordered Abu Bakr to lead the prayer?" he said, referring to the period before his death when Muhammad was too weak to lead the congregational prayers.

"We know it," they answered.

"Then which of you would willingly take precedence over him?" Umar asked.

"God forbid that we should take precedence over him!" they responded.

Umar then seized the hand of Abu Bakr and pledged allegiance to him. All the others likewise pledged their allegiance to Abu Bakr.

Muslims have a concept called *bayah* in Arabic, which means "oath of allegiance" and refers to the act of a leader being accepted into a community. When Abu Bakr accepted the *bayah* from the Muslims in Medina, he praised God and then delivered the following speech:

**I have been given the authority over you, and I am not the best of you. If I do well, help me; and if I do wrong, set me right. Sincere regard for truth is loyalty and disregard for truth is treachery. The weak among you shall be strong with me until I have secured his rights, God willing; and the strong among you shall be weak with me until I have wrested from him the rights of others, God willing. Obey me as long as I obey God and His Messenger. But if I disobey God and His Messenger, you owe me no obedience. Arise for prayer, may God have mercy upon you!**

Abu Bakr became the first caliph of the *ummah*. He was succeeded by three of Muhammad's other close companions, Umar, Uthman, and Ali. These four leaders are known as the *rashidun*, or the rightly guided caliphs. They were chosen by the community based on their merit, as well as on their close association with Muhammad.

# The Rightly guided ones
## Medina, 632 to 661

Abu Bakr found himself the leader of a community the likes of which Arabia had never seen before. For the first time, the tribes were united by their faith. Each respected the command given by Muhammad and the Quran not to attack one another. The Muslims then turned their attention elsewhere, looking to expand their community.

Expeditions into non-Muslim lands served several purposes. They gave the young *ummah* a unifying activity and cemented the position of the caliph as a military leader. The title *Amir al-Mu'mineen* (Commander of the Faithful) conferred on Umar bin al-Khattab, the second caliph, attests to the military aspect of the caliphs.

Before his death, Muhammad had begun to educate non-Muslim leaders from beyond the peninsula about Islam, sending them cordial letters of invitation into the faith. After his death, his closest companions continued the task of educating others about Islam and taking Muhammad's message with them into non-Muslim lands.

The expeditions blossomed during Umar's ten-year rule from 634 to 644. By 644 Muslims controlled the lands of Egypt, Palestine, Syria, Iraq, and Persia. Under the rule of the third caliph, Uthman, the Muslims captured much of the North African coast. Just twenty years after their first battle—the battle of Badr—the Muslims found themselves leaders of a large and diverse empire. At the time, Islam was still very much an Arab religion as there was no effort yet made to convert the non-Arabic conquered peoples to the Islamic faith.

The *rashidun* were respectful of other faiths, especially the *ahl al-*

*kitab*, or People of the Book (Jews and Christians), who are mentioned in the Quran. During Umar's rule, he invited about seventy Jewish families to return to live in Jerusalem after they had been banished from the city by the Romans. Once, when it was time for the Islamic prayer, the Christian patriarch of the city invited Umar to pray in the Church of the Holy Sepulcher, but Umar refused. He was aware that if he prayed there, he might set a precedent and Muslims might appropriate the Christian site for their own worship. So he prayed outside the great church instead.

Minorities living under Muslim rule were allowed to retain their legal systems except for certain criminal laws. Arab soldiers settled in garrison towns built outside the main towns and the conquered lands were left to local landowners who paid rent to the Islamic state.

Under the law of the desert, Arab tribes extended protection to weaker groups who were clients of the more powerful tribe. Once local Jews, Christians, and others came under Muslim protection, they could not be raided or attacked and were free to practice their religion. They became protected subjects (*dhimmis*) of the Islamic state. In return for protection and good treatment, the *dhimmis* paid a tax called the *jizyah*. There were times when, for one reason or another, the Muslim rulers couldn't protect their subjects and returned the *jizyah* to the subject people.

In 644 Umar was assassinated by a Persian prisoner of war, and Uthman was elected as the third caliph. The *ummah* prospered for the first several years of his rule and saw some significant developments. One of the most important, perhaps, was the completion of a written Quran.

The Quran was originally an oral recitation, and there were many among Muhammad's companions who had memorized it in its entirety. But many of these learned individuals were growing old and dying. The companions of Muhammad, particularly Abu Bakr and Aishah, recognized the danger of losing the Quran exactly as it had been revealed to Muhammad. They set about collecting all the written verses of the Quran, which various people had in their possession on stones, leather, and papyrus, and organizing them, with the goal of creating one complete text. There was initially some opposition to this proposal, because it had not been initiated by Muhammad, but the project continued nonetheless. Once the Quran was compiled, it was checked and rechecked by those who had memorized it and was ultimately left in the care of Hafsa, one of Muhammad's widows.

During Uthman's rule, from 644 to 656, people of different cultures, languages, and customs started converting to Islam, and Uthman saw the necessity of copying the Quran and distributing the one authentic version throughout the caliphate. This is the Arabic version that is in print today.

At the same time, on the frontiers of the caliphate, the Muslims seized Cyprus and continued across North Africa. To the east, they went as far as the Indian subcontinent. But despite a succession of victories, the first *fitnah*, or turmoil, arose in the Muslim *ummah* when Uthman was assassinated in 656 by a group of soldiers.

Ali was the obvious choice as successor, as he had been one of Muhammad's closest companions as well as his cousin and son-in-law. Many Muslims believed that Ali should have been the first caliph instead of Abu Bakr, and they were happy to see Ali finally ascend to the position. The first ideological split within the *ummah* occurred over this development, as some believed that the caliph should be a member of Muhammad's family and others felt that should not be a requirement.

Meanwhile, Muawiyyah, a man from Uthman's own clan, the Umayyad family, had been appointed governor in Damascus, and had a growing interest in being chosen caliph. Ali's rule was not supported in Syria where Muawiyyah led the opposition movement.

When Ali assumed the post of caliph and settled in Kufa, a city in Iraq, Muawiyyah challenged his rule by sending troops into Iraq and declaring himself caliph. Ali and Muawiyyah came to an agreement, but some of Ali's followers withdrew their support claiming that by not crushing Muawiyyah, Ali had betrayed the ideals of justice as set down in the Quran. This group of dissenters became known as the Kharajites (seceders), and Ali attempted to quiet them. But in 661 Ali was assassinated by a Kharajite.

Muawiyyah then established the first Islamic dynasty and shifted the capital of the *ummah* from Medina to Damascus. Many saw this geographic shift as mirroring an ideological shift away from the world of the Prophet. The rule of the *rashidun* had lasted thirty-four years before Muslims came under the leadership of a dynasty.

The days of the *rashidun* and the expansion of the caliphate are seen by Muslims as a sign that the Muslim people were living in tune with God's laws. All four initial caliphs are regarded as being just and noble who ruled in the spirit of the Quran and exercised a strict sense of social justice. Many lamented the end of their era of rule.

## The first Muslim Dynasty
### Damascus, 661 to 750

Under Muawiyyah's rule, the Umayyad dynasty was born. Arabic became the official language in Muslim lands, and Islamic coins bearing Quranic phrases were issued. The first major Islamic monument, the Dome of the Rock, was completed in Jerusalem in 691 and set the precedent for the distinctive architectural features associated with Islamic buildings, including the use of domes and verses of the Quran inscribed as decorative script. During the Umayyad dynasty, Islam spread eastward into north India and western China as well as west across North Africa and into Spain.

During this time, the *ummah* became divided into various social strata with the Arab minority forming a privileged class. In reaction, Islamic scholars pushed for more stringent applications of the Quran. Later, the field of *fiqh*, the science of Islamic law based on the Quran and hadith, emerged. These movements had popular appeal as dissatisfaction grew among Muslims unhappy with the distribution of power and among non-Muslims disgruntled by the lack of opportunities available to them.

Members of the Abbasid family, originally from Mecca, began to capitalize on this dissatisfaction by emphasizing their closeness to Muhammad and tracing their descent through Muhammad's uncle Abbas.

## The Abbasid Caliphate
### Baghdad, 750 to 935

The Abbasids came to power by slaughtering as many of the ruling Umayyads as they could. One member of the Umayyad family, a young prince called Abd al-Rahman, managed to slip away and set up a satellite caliphate based in Cordova, Spain. The Abbasids meanwhile quashed any opposition to their rule and moved the capital from Damascus to Baghdad, where they set up an absolute monarchy.

The Abbasid dynasty proved successful on many fronts—politically, financially, and culturally. During its nearly two-hundred-year rule, rulers presided over a flowering of the arts and learning. Although the empire eventually broke up into smaller, independent provinces, the Abbasids sought to establish equality for the empire's various ethnic groups and provinces. The rulers realized that the fabric of the Muslim population had changed since the days of Muhammad and the *rashidun*. Converts to Islam were becoming the majority, and these new Muslims came to the faith from many different cultures, bringing their old practices with them. The Abbasids thus sought to establish an officially and universally recognized form of Islam to regulate the spiritual and daily lives of Muslims.

## The Golden Age
### 750 to 1250

A cultural renaissance began during Abbasid rule, a flowering of the arts, science, and philosophy that spread from the eastern reaches of the empire to the borders of Europe. The accomplishments made during this time affected the course and scope of modern civilization. The Islamic golden age was spurred by a simple directive found in the Quran: seek knowledge.

Muslim scholars traveled to all corners of the known world—China, India, Iran, Egypt, Greece, and Iraq—collecting the knowledge, current and historical, of the greatest civilizations. They translated scientific and philosophical texts into Arabic. They then analyzed the translations and either accepted or rejected the thoughts and insights put forward in the texts. Muslim scholars used aspects of this new learning to advance their own thinking and the intellectual development of the Muslim world as a whole.

As a result of these activities, the Muslim world became embroiled in various debates, challenges, and rebuttals, as the written word joined oral discourses as a means of relaying and transmitting ideas. Having learned the Chinese art of papermaking, the Muslims

**A display of traditional writing implements and equipment from a Quranic school. Due to the scarcity of wood and paper, pupils often wrote on the shoulder blade of a cow, using a damp cloth to erase the texts they had recorded there. Also shown are a glass inkwell, a reed pen, and an oil lap.**

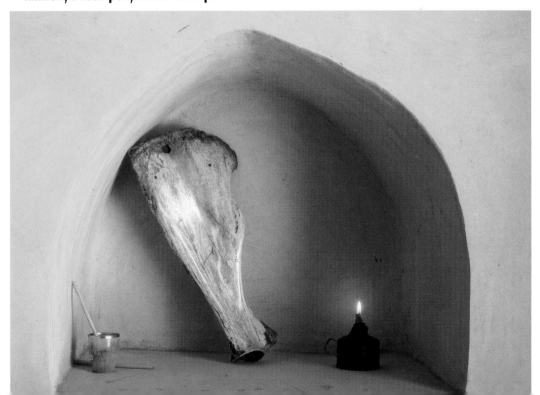

turned paper into the standard medium for written communication. Professional manuscript copiers called *waraqeen* could copy a few hundred pages in a matter of hours. Bookshops sprang up in the major cities, such as Baghdad, Damascus, and Cairo, starting in the eighth century, and a publishing industry developed. At its peak, tens of thousands of books were published each year.

The intellectual debates that arose during this age of cultural expansion were dynamic and stretched over centuries as one scholar responded to the ideas of another. The debates led to the development of different groups and schools of thinking and ultimately fostered the evolution of new philosophies based on the wisdom of the Quran.

Institutions of learning also arose during this time, as students flowed out of the mosques, the traditional place of learning, and into colleges called *madrassas* and universities called *jamias*. In 973 Al-Azhar, a great mosque, was dedicated in Cairo. Soon thereafter, Al-Azhar University, the world's first university, was started. It remains one of the best universities in the Muslim world.

The first hospital was also established on the banks of the Euphrates River, where clean water was collected upstream and waste sent downstream. Soon Baghdad alone boasted sixty hospitals. Doctors studied optometry and communicable diseases. They were the first to diagnose smallpox and measles and understand how these diseases were spread. One of the greatest Muslim scholars, Ibn Sīnā, wrote a medical textbook of fourteen volumes that was used in the Western world until the sixteenth century.

In the field of mathematics, the Muslims developed the system of algebra and made great strides in trigonometry. A major motivation for this research was to find more accurate methods of dividing land in observance with the complicated Quranic stipulations on inheritance. In the field of astronomy, the astrolabe was improved to chart the precise time of the sunrise and sunset, as well as the start of the fast of Ramadan, which begins when the new moon is sighted at the onset of the ninth month of the Islamic calendar.

**The Sultan Hassan Mosque is one of the many distinctive centers of worship found in Cairo, Egypt.**

Muslims were also active in the social sciences, including psychology, history, ethnography, archaeology, and geography. They were tireless travelers and effective documentarians. Some of the earliest encyclopedias were compiled during this period and contained observations and analyses by Islamic travelers. Cartographers created maps that included lines of latitude and longitude, details about tides and the directions of prevailing winds. By the tenth century, an organized postal system—the world's first—had been put in place.

Islamic architecture evolved during the Abbasid dynasty, and the results can still be appreciated today in the Moroccan city of Fez, the mud houses of Yemen's capital city Sana, and the mosques of Cairo. Town planning developed to accommodate large populations that swelled throughout the tenth and eleventh centuries. Towns were often built beside rivers that supplied drinking water and carried away waste. These communities were compact and organized into neighborhoods centering on mosques and universities. The souk, or marketplace, was the commercial center. Muslims at this time also introduced the idea of protected zones where development was forbidden to better conserve natural resources and wildlife.

The Islamic world is also renowned for its art whose roots lie in the days of the Abbasid dynasty. The depiction of human figures is not common in Islamic art, due to the belief that only God creates. Instead, Muslims took calligraphy, geometric designs, and decorative arts in general to an extraordinary degree of complexity and grace in the areas of glasswork; metalwork; carpet, cloth, and tapestry weaving; book illustration; and miniature painting.

Until the 1600s, the general flow of knowledge was from the Islamic world westward. Arabic was the language of science, philosophy, letters, and arts. English words that originated in Arabic— such as *sugar, coffee, sofa, algebra,* and *assassin*—are reminders of the range, influence, and innovations of the Islamic civilization that flourished from the eighth to the thirteenth centuries.

## Disintegration of the caliphate

No large empire based on agriculture can thrive forever, and gradually the Abbasids began to lose control of the peripheral provinces, such as the caliphate in Spain. There was growing and widespread awareness that despite the successful spread of Islamic rule and the Muslims' astounding cultural and intellectual achievements, the caliphate itself did not live up to the standards of the Quran. By the tenth century, it became clear that the Abbasid empire was in decline. Most Muslims saw this decline as an emancipation for the *ummah*.

Over the next two hundred years, the caliphate became more of a symbol than a reality and the Muslim world splintered into small dynasties and regional rulers—a political development that was actually more in keeping with the egalitarian spirit of the Quran. The Shiite Fatimids took control of Egypt and ruled much of North Africa, Arabia, Syria, and Palestine. Turkish army officers (called *amirs*) established power in Iraq, Iran, and central Asia. Seljuk Turks, a nomadic Turkish tribe and converts to Islam who hailed from central Asia, made a special arrangement with the caliph to act as his lieutenants throughout the Islamic world. Despite the cultural diversity of the regional rulers and the range of their various often far-flung realms, most acknowledged the authority of the Abbasid caliphate, at least nominally. Still change was inevitable, and over the next five hundred years, the Islamic world saw a series of undulating empires rise and fall.

## crusaders and mongols
### 1095 to 1405

With the breakup of the caliphate, individual regional rulers asserted themselves. They were often preoccupied with fighting one another, and the lands of the Near East became vulnerable to invasion. The Crusaders—Christians from western Europe acting on the orders of Pope Urban II to capture the Holy Land after the Seljuk Turks had made advances into Byzantine territory—attacked Jerusalem in 1099, massacring its inhabitants and establishing states in the region. It took the Muslims almost a hundred years to drive the Crusaders out. In 1187 a Kurdish general called Salah ad-Din succeeded in reclaiming Jerusalem.

The next serious challenge the Muslims faced was from the nomadic warriors who came riding out of the steppes of Mongolia. The arrival of the Mongols proved to be a turning point in Islamic history. Never before had such significant areas of the Muslim world been so soundly defeated. The Mongols were intent on building an empire, and their military superiority lay in their tribal unity, strict discipline, ability to endure hardship, heavy but mobile armaments, and their use of tactics such as spies and acts of terror.

Baghdad fell to the Mongols in 1258 and with it fell the Abbasid dynasty. The invaders razed the city and set the libraries on fire, causing centuries of learning to go up in smoke. Survivors fled east to India and west to Egypt. The Mongols sacked cities across the region and created an empire spanning from China in the east to Constantinople in the west.

Although the Mongols originally had shamanic traditions, their policy of building on local cultures led them to adopt Buddhism when they conquered China, and, after extending their empire into the Muslim world, to adopt the Islamic faith.

The Mongols set about rebuilding the cities they had destroyed, bringing new energy and ideas of expansion to the Muslim world. But damage had been done and in the haze of the smoldering libraries of Islam's great cities, the Golden Age drew to a close.

With the fall of the Abbasid caliphate, a new polity emerged in the Islamic world. Rulers were not Arabs or descendants or companions of Muhammad; neither did they rule by consensus. The Mongols ruled in Iran and the eastern edges of the Muslim world, and the exchange of goods and ideas with East Asia thrived. In 1250 the Mamluks, a military corps of former slaves mostly from central Asia and southern Russia, took power in Egypt and Syria, and the westernmost parts of the Islamic world saw a series of dynasties rise and fall.

## closing the gates
1200s onward

It is impossible to pinpoint what caused the decline of Abbasid glory and the intellectual setbacks. Some historians say that Mongol destruction made the Islamic world aware of its own vulnerability and caused it to turn inward. Others attribute the downfall to the corruption of leaders and to ongoing internal divisions.

Others point toward the loss of Spain. Internal fighting in al-Andalus and corruption in the far-flung capital of Cordoba had led to the loss of all but the small city-state of Granada. When the Muslim sultan Boabdil of Granada handed the Christian king Ferdinand the keys to the city of Granada in 1492, he ended eight hundred years of Muslim rule in Spain.

Still others blame the *ulema* (religious scholars) for the intellectual decline. The *ulema* had controlled civil society since the caliphate broke into independently ruled regions in the early 900s. These regions were militarily controlled by the emirs, and the *ulema* governed the intellectual, religious, and social affairs of the population. With the proliferation and distribution of books and the growing distance between an author and his ideas, the *ulema* became worried that texts, especially the Quran, would be vulnerable to a range of interpretations. The *ulema* were additionally concerned about maintaining their own power and influence. They began to attempt to control and curtail intellectual inquiry.

Whatever the cause, over the course of a hundred years the outward-looking, knowledge-seeking attitude of the population shifted. A more reductionist and isolated position generally prevailed.

## ottoman empire
### Fourteenth century to 1922

By the late fourteenth century, a family that ruled one of the small states that had emerged from the Mongols' declining empire was becoming increasingly powerful. This was the Osmanli family, otherwise known as the Ottomans. They were Turkish-speaking nomads who had converted to Islam. The age of Ottoman rule began with the conquest of Constantinople in 1453, a city that had long been considered a great prize due to its strategic location at the crossroads of Europe and Asia. The city was renamed Istanbul in 1930. The Ottoman rulers laid claim to the Islamic caliphate, after pushing out the last Abbasids living under the Mamluks in Egypt. The Ottomans did not require travel documents of any Muslim arriving from outside the empire. They also provided the Islamic world with a political center and supported Islamic orthodoxy. The Ottomans developed an efficient military body and spurred economic growth by invading other territories. They coexisted with two other large empires, the Safavids in Iran and the Mughals in India.

Ottoman success was aided, in part, by the acquisition of gunpowder. At its peak in the sixteenth century, the empire ruled much of the Middle East, North Africa, and what are now the Balkan states and Hungary, and its population was estimated to be between 30 and 50 million. Despite the overall cultural and intellectual decline of the realm, Islam was, at the peak of the Ottoman empire, a formidable political force in the world.

But by the end of the eighteenth century, the Ottoman empire, was, in many respects, a mirage. Although the Ottomans had mastered warfare and the acquisition of new territories, the rulers in Constantinople were losing control of the fringe provinces; outside the capital, local rulers were often corrupt, taxes were barely collected, and trade had declined.

As the Ottoman empire began its decline in the late 1700s, the Western world was gathering momentum. The Ottomans realized that reform was necessary to survive and they began to institute changes in the empire, such as importing European instructors to teach languages and new Western sciences. These attempts at Westernization led to stirrings of Turkish nationalism and culminated in the creation of a secular Turkish state under Mustafa Kemal Ataturk in 1924 after the Ottoman empire was dissolved at the end of World War I.

Along with the Ottomans, two other absolute monarchies ruled at around the same time: the Shiite Safavids in Iran (1501–1732) and the Moguls (1483–1858) in India.

The Safavids established the first Shiite empire. Shiism is one of the two major branches of Islam. The leaders imported Shiite *ulema* from the Arab world and installed them in *madrassas* where they could teach an orthodox form of Shiism.

The Moguls ruled with tolerance for the other religions in India and built some spectacular buildings, including the Taj Mahal in Agra and the Red Fort in Delhi. Akbar led the Mogul empire at its peak (1556–1605). His reign was characterized by tolerance and cooperation with the Hindus and people of other faiths. During this time, the expansion of Islam continued as traders and mystic wanderers (known as Sufis) brought the faith east to Southeast Asia and north into Europe.

## The West Arrives

As the Muslim world saw the rise and fall of one monarchy after another, western Europe was gradually emerging as a powerful force on the global scene.

Beginning with India, in the 1700s, and sweeping across the Middle East to the west coast of Africa, various Western nations entered one Islamic country after another. France occupied Algeria and Tunisia; England ruled Egypt and Sudan; and Russia controlled of parts of central Asia and the Persian empire. England was involved in the development of the Arabian Gulf sheikhdoms (including what is today the United Arab Emirates, Qatar, Bahrain, and Oman) and later helped them develop the institutions needed to harness oil and other resources.

The defeat of the Ottomans, who were allied with the central European powers in World War I, as well as rising secular Turkish nationalism, led to the breakup of the Ottoman empire at the end of the war. Parts of the territory were divided between England and France.

The process of colonization had a profound effect on the Islamic world and has colored the way many Muslims view the West. Even after the various colonizing Western nations relinquished their foreign holdings, they left various conflicts in their wake. England left India fractured into Hindu India and Muslim Pakistan, in 1947, and facing the violence that ensued. The creation of the secular Jewish state in Palestine in 1948, backed by the United Nations (UN) and with British support, caused the exile of thousands of Palestinians, Mulsim decendants of the Arabs who had inhabited the region.

## The modern ıslαmic state

The twentieth century collision between the Muslim world and the West resulted in the creation of a patchwork of politically autonomous states with Muslim majorities. For the first time in their history, Muslims were not considered members of an overarching caliphate. Instead they were split into the citizens of nations that were, in some cases, created without regard to regional or ethnic differences. The region known as Kurdistan, for example, was divided starting in 1923 among Turkey, Syria, and Iraq. The large region known as Sham was split into Syria, Jordan, Lebanon, and Palestine. Islamic countries were now faced with the daunting task of building themselves, sometimes from scratch, into modern nation-states that had to establish their identities on an international level. Perhaps the biggest issues these modern states encountered involved questions of nationalism, democracy, and secularism and the role of religion in the governing and judicial structure.

Since the days of the Prophet Muhammad until the end of the Ottoman empire, Muslims had belonged, at least loosely, to one community based on faith—the Islamic *ummah,* with one caliph. They were Muslims first and citizens second. Now they were faced with fitting themselves into definite regional, but somewhat arbitrary, boundaries.

The concept of democracy poses a challenge to Islam by the simple fact that in a democracy the people are considered sovereign. Most democracies have a republican form of government in which citizens express their will through elected representatives. But according to Islam, God is the only sovereign. Muslim jurists pondered the question of how human-created laws could be reconciled with the laws that God laid down in the Quran.

Although the Quran does not specify a particular form of government that Muslims should institute, it does identify various social and political values that it should embody. Among these are justice, social cooperation, and a consultative method of governance. Many Muslims argue that the elemental components of a democracy— the institution of the vote, the division of power, an independent judiciary, and a free press—are concordant with Islamic values of governance.

Those Muslims in support of democracy point to the democratic principles of Islam, such as the concepts of *bayah* (oath of allegiance), *shura* (consultation), and the historical fact that Muhammad did not assign a successor but left the decision to the community. They also note that all four *rashidun* were elected by the consensus of the community and that Muhammad himself wrote a constitution. Furthermore, Islam is a religion based on justice, and thus, the pursuit of justice is the responsibility of every human being. In the words of Islamic scholar Khaled Abou El Fadl, "Democracy does not ensure justice. But it does establish a basis for pursuing justice and thus for fulfilling a fundamental responsibility assigned by God to each one of us."

During the creation of the modern nations, Muslims had to face an integral element of democracy, that is, the separation of church and state. Islamic concepts such a *tawhid*, the absolute oneness of God, and the unity of everything in existence mean that the exclusion of religion from politics, or from any other arena of life, is impossible. But rather than rejecting the idea of separation of church and state, many Muslims instead understand the separation of church and state

**Indonesia has the world's largest Muslim population. These women attend morning prayers during Eid al-Fitr at Parangkusumo Beach outside Yogyakarta in central Java, one of many islands that make up the nation.**

to refer to the government not forcing a particular religion on the people. Another term for the separation of church and state, then, is freedom of religion, itself an Islamic concept and one addressed in the Quran that states there is to be no enforced religion. (Quran 2:256)

Another result of an increased awareness of the West in the Muslim world was the rise of significant thinkers and ideologues who were motivated by questions of how to modernize their countries. Most attempts to merge modern Western ideas of democracy with Islamic societies have been, unfortunately, more superficial than substantial, and parts of the Muslim world are still searching for an ideal Islamic political system that works in modern times.

Some states with majority Muslim populations have secular or socialist governments (such as Indonesia and Turkey). Other states are governed by Islamic law (such as Saudi Arabia). Today, there are about fifty independent countries with a Muslim majority, and many other countries have large Muslim populations. Collectively, these countries are generally known as the Muslim or Islamic world.

Many Muslims dream of a united Islamic world, like in the days of the *rashidun*. In the name of political, economic, social, cultural, and scientific cooperation among the states in the Islamic world, King Faisal of Saudi Arabia established the Organization of the Islamic Conference in 1969 with the aim of strengthening Islamic solidarity.

## Backlash

With the spread of Western values and modernity throughout the Muslim world over the last fifty years, in places a spike of conservative and often extremist values has risen in response. Some people in the Muslim world feel at odds with the West and see the military actions of the United States and Great Britain in the Middle East as another instance of the colonialism of the past and motivated by the desire for oil and strategic interests.

The more extreme individuals and groups, claiming to be acting in the name of the religion, advocate using violence and terror to retaliate against what they see as wrongs inflicted by the Western world and the encroachment of undesirable Western values. But only a fringe minority of Muslims are involved in such tactics; the vast majority of the Muslim world decries the use of such violent acts as suicide bombing (suicide is forbidden in the Quran) and the killing of civilians (also forbidden). Most Muslims are devastated by these actions being conducted in the name of their religion and feel that proponents of terror and violence have seriously deviated from true Islam, which is characterized by peace, wisdom, and high moral values. The religious leaders, people, nongovernmental organizations (NGOs), and governments of many Muslim countries are working hard to find solutions to end the violence and create understanding as Islam and the world enter the intial decades of the twenty-first century.

# three

# CREED

## muhammad's message to humanity

The Quran states that people were created to worship the One who created them; this is the purpose of human life. A Muslim endeavors to be the best human being possible in the eyes of God by following the Quran and the example set by the life of Muhammad.

A simple way to understand Islam is to think of the Quran as the message, God as the author of the message, and Muhammad as the message bearer.

The Islamic religion is built on specific beliefs and practices that must be accepted and followed for a person to be considered an actively practicing Muslim. The goal of the observant Muslim is to perfect these practices to obtain a deepening understanding of God as a divine presence. As Muslims devote themselves to their faith, they experience three progressive categories of spiritual awareness:

*islam:* **the conscious and deliberate surrender to God**
*iman:* **the deepening certainty in the existence of God; and**
*ihsan:* **perfecting oneself in terms of faith, action, and humanity.**

To illustrate these concepts, the following story about Muhammad offers an apt summary of the main beliefs and practices of the Islamic religion.

**One day, the Prophet was seated with his companions when a**

stranger of exceedingly black hair and exceedingly white clothes approached the group. None of the companions knew him, yet he had no signs of travel on him. The stranger sat down knee to knee opposite the Prophet and placed his palms on the Prophet's thighs. Then he asked Muhammad, "Oh Muhammad, tell me, what is islam (surrender)?" The Prophet answered him, listing what are known as the Five Pillars: "Islam is to testify that there is no god but God and that Muhammad is God's Messenger, to perform the daily prayer, bestow alms, fast during Ramadan, and make, if you can, the pilgrimage to the Ka'bah in Mecca." To the surprise of Muhammad's companions, this stranger responded by saying, "You are correct."

Next he asked "What is iman (faith)?" to which the Prophet responded by listing the items of belief: in God, in the angels, in all the books, in all the messengers, and in the last day, life after death, and that no good or bad comes to a person but by God's providence. Again the questioner said, "You have spoken truly."

Then he asked, "Tell me, what is ihsan (excellence)?" To which the Prophet answered, "Ihsan is to worship God as if you see Him; and if you don't see Him, then worship Him with the conviction that He sees you." The man replied again, "You are correct."

Then the stranger stood up and took his leave. After his departure, the Prophet asked his companions, "Do you know who that was?" They answered in the negative. "That was the angel Gabriel, and he came to teach you your religion."

The fundamentals of Islam, as this story relates, are contained in the beliefs and the practices, also called the Five Pillars, of Islam.

# the five beliefs

There are five primary articles of belief in the Islamic faith. Together they make up the philosophical fabric of the religion.

## 1. Belief in God

Muslims believe that there is only one God, or *Allah* in Arabic. God is unique, without a partner, and beyond description, beyond the boundaries of human conception. The Quran describes God through metaphor and parables:

> **God is the light of the heavens and the earth. The parable of his light is, as it were, that of a niche containing a lamp; the lamp is enclosed in glass, the glass shining like a radiant star, lit from a blessed tree—an olive tree that is neither of the east nor of the west—the oil of which is so bright that it gives light of itself even though fire has not touched it. Light upon light! God guides to his light whom he will, and propounds parables to men since God alone has full knowledge of things." (Quran 24:35)**

To Muslims, God is known as the Most Merciful. Anecdotes of this attribute are threaded into every aspect of Islam. The Arabic word for "mercy," *rahma,* is derived from a word meaning "womb" and signifies both the nurturing a child receives in the womb and the love a mother has for her child. All creation is said to be embedded in the mercy of God, epitomized by God's words "My mercy prevails over my wrath" and the chanting of the angels closest to the Divine.

Muslims believe that everything that exists, continues to exist, and ceases to exist is dependant on God. God's existence is without a beginning or an end. The oneness and uniqueness of God, known as *tawhid,* is the central message of the Quran.

Why the singularity of God is stressed in the Islamic faith stems from the fact that the message of Muhammad was first introduced to

# referring to god

Muslims refer to God in Arabic as *Allah subhana wa talla* ("God, the most exalted and high").

In the Quran, God refers to himself in various pronouns such as I, we, and he. Islamic scholars have proposed that the reason for these several pronouns may be so that the reader does not form an image in his or her mind about who or what God is.

Muslims also believe that God is neither male nor female. But since there is no personal pronoun in either Arabic or English that distinguishes beyond gender, it is easiest and most common to refer to God as he, rather than she. Muslims try to see past this limitation in human language.

a polytheistic culture. The pre-Islamic Arabs had various gods that they worshipped through the use of idols. In addition, for Muslims God's singularity is diminished not only through idols. Setting up a "partner" to God also refers to concepts, ideologies, material acquisitions, worldly pursuits, and even one's own ego. If the focus of Islam is surrender to God, then this means that God should be a person's highest priority and nothing else should come close in terms of importance.

This preeminence of God for the Muslim believer begins to explain the nature and frequency of the Islamic canonical prayer—five times a day. One's worldly life is suspended during prayer, as priority and focus are given to God alone.

## 2. Belief in the Messengers

Muslims believe that God communicates to humanity through specially chosen human beings, called prophets or messengers. Prophets have been sent to all peoples in all cultures and at all times. The prophets have similar life stories in that they are commonly rejected by the majority but have managed to capture the attention of a small percentage of faithful. Some prophets are persecuted or put to death. Each one had a distinct personality and a particular emphasis but their essential message has been the same: that is, to recognize and worship God and live a righteous and moral life. The critical presence of the prophets is stated in the following verse: "And indeed, within every civilization, have we raised up an apostle (entrusted him with this message): 'Worship God and shun the powers of evil!'" (Quran 16:36)

The Quran mentions twenty-five prophets by name, starting with Adam, the first human being and prophet, and including Noah, Abraham, Ishmael, Isaac, Jacob, Joseph, David, Solomon, Moses, Aaron, Job, Jonah, John the Baptist, Jesus, and Muhammad. The Quran also states that many more prophets existed than are named in the Quran, thus leaving room for the possibility that spiritual leaders can be found in other cultures and eras: "And indeed (Oh Muhammad), we sent forth apostles before your time; some of them we have mentioned to you (in the Quran), and some of them we have not mentioned to you . . ." (Quran 40:78)

Muslims believe that the prophets are true bearers of God's messages, and the Quran tells people to make no distinction between them. (Quran 2:285) But Muslims believe that Muhammad was the last prophet and that God will send no other prophets until the end of time.

The Quran mentions that the prophets, like individual human beings, are not equally endowed with attributes: "Some of these apostles we have endowed more highly than others: among them were such as were spoken to by God, and some he has raised yet higher. And we vouchsafed to Jesus, the son of Mary, all evidence of the truth, and strengthened him with holy inspiration." (Quran 2:253)

Muslims believe that Jesus was a prophet but not the son of God, because they do not believe that God has offspring like humans do. They also do not believe that Jesus was crucified but only appeared to have been.

One of the most important traits of a prophet is that he or she is always human, thereby providing a living example of the heights individuals are capable of reaching. If a prophet was an angel, mortal human beings could never aspire to following that angelic prophet's example.

Given his human nature, a prophet cannot know the unknowable except through divine revelation. The Quran instructs Muhammad to clarify this to his people: "Say: 'It is not within my power to bring benefit to, or avert harm from, myself, except as God may please. And if I knew that which is beyond the reach of human perception, abundant good fortune would surely have fallen to me, and no evil would ever have touched me. I am nothing but a warner, and a herald of glad tidings unto people who will believe.'" (Quran 7:188)

A prophet cannot transcend the laws of nature through miracles; miracles are impossible without divine intervention. The Quran instructs Muhammad to inform his people, "Say: Miracles are in the power of God alone." (Quran 6:109)

Miracles, found in the life stories of most of the prophets, serve to prove that they are true prophets. Miracles are not emphasized in Muhammad's life story, although he did perform some. Rather, the emphasis of Muhammad's teachings is on the miracle of the Quran itself and of how it was revealed to him. Islamic scholars have compared the passing of the Quran from God through Muhammad to the divine conception of Jesus through his mother Mary. God revealed the complex and poetic Quran through the unlettered Muhammad; God breathed the soul of Jesus into the virgin womb of Mary. Muslims see the descent of the Quran as the real miracle of the Islamic faith.

### 3. Belief in the Messages

Muslims believe in the validity of the messages brought by the prophets: "Indeed, all this has indeed been said in the earlier revelations." (Quran 87:18) They also believe that the Quran reiterates and clarifies principles laid down in previous scriptures, such as the Torah, the Jewish scriptures that are also referred to as the Old Testament.

The Quran, consisting of verses called signs or *ayahs* in Arabic and arranged into 114 chapters, is the essence of Islam. Muhammad's role was to reveal and explain it. The Quran was originally an oral recitation, and Muhammad memorized each verse as it was revealed to him. Additionally, many of his companions memorized the entire Quran, some of them writing it down as well.

In keeping with tradition, people around the world memorize the entire Quran—sometimes by the age of seven. Due to its rhythmical quality, the Quran is known to lend itself easily to memorization. When a student memorizes the Quran in the schools of Mecca, Medina, and elsewhere, that student receives a certificate in which the chain of transmission is recorded. The name of the student is placed last; above the student's name is the name of the teacher; and above the teacher's name is the teacher's teacher. This chain continues through the line of teachers. At the top of the chain—the first name on the list—is the Prophet Muhammad. He received the Quran from the angel Gabriel who received it from God.

## 4. Belief in the Angels

Muslims believe in the existence of angels as beings of light and as part of the unseen world. Angels are always among people although they cannot be seen unless they take the form of a human or other material being. An example of an angel that assumed a visible form is Gabriel who took the form of a man when he visited Muhammad while he was sitting with his companions and when Gabriel appeared to Mary to tell her that she would bear a son. Unlike human beings, angels do not have their own free will. Thus, humans can reach beyond the heights of the angels—or fall below the station of animals—depending on their intentions and deeds.

According to Islamic theology, angels were created before human beings. When God created Adam, he asked all the angels to prostrate themselves before him, which they did—all except Iblis, or Satan. Satan then vowed to lead human beings astray from the path of righteousness until the Day of Judgment, when all souls will stand before God and have their lives judged. God agreed to let Satan act as an agent of evil to test people's faith.

Angels were created by God to worship him and, by executing his commands, to help with the functioning of the universe. Apart from worshipping God and encircling his throne, the angels have several other specific tasks including bringing messages from God to his prophets and emissaries on earth. This task is reserved for Gabriel. They protect human beings, as stated in the Quran: "For each there are angels in succession before and behind him; they guard him by command of God." (Quran 13:11)

Angels record the deeds and intentions of human beings in minute detail. Muslims believe that there is an angel on the right side and the left side of each person who records everything that person does. This record is to be read when the person is called to account on the Day of Judgment. Each *salaat* (Islamic prayer) ends with the words *salaam aleikum* ("peace be upon you"), said over each shoulder to the angels on either side. Angels also take charge of the people of heaven and of hell.

When a person dies, 'Azra'il, the angel of death, collects the human soul. The Quran tells Muhammad: "Say: One day the angel of death, who has been given charge of you, will take your souls, and then to your Sustainer will you be brought back." (Quran 32:11)

The angel Mika'il (Michael) blows a horn marking the significant events in the soul's existence. He issues three blasts: the first at death, the second to awaken people from the slumber of death, and the third at resurrection.

## 5. Belief in the Afterlife

The Quran describes what happens after a human life expires. Time and again the Quran admonishes people who refuse to believe that a day will come when creation will come to an end. Each human soul will be raised from the dead to meet God, each person's actions judged, and the station of that soul's afterlife determined.

At the time of death, a moment determined by God, the angel of death comes to take the soul. The soul is taken to its resting place in the grave. There it stays until the Day of Resurrection, when all souls will be awakened from the slumber of death to await their meeting with God. Next comes the Day of Judgment when all souls will be evaluated in terms of their actions and intentions on earth. Good deeds will be weighed against negative ones, as recorded by the angels. Muslims believe that God will ask each person whether or not they acknowledged him and his messengers and will review how each person spent the moments of his or her life.

From the moment of this review onward, good deeds will bring unimaginable pleasure, and negative deeds will bring unimaginable pain. The souls of the people who acknowledged God and lived a good life—who were merciful toward others, generous, truthful, patient, and pious—will enter the gates of paradise. Those who denied or ignored the existence of God and who were arrogant, miserly, oppressive, unjust, and untruthful will descend into the fires of hell.

Belief in the afterlife is an important aspect of Islamic faith because it not only tests a person's trust in what the Quran and Muhammad says, it also affects how a Muslim lives his or her life on earth. The quality of the experience of the afterlife differs depending on how individuals lived in relation to God, others, themselves, and the earth and its creatures.

The Quran describes the ingredients of living a good life, also called the *sirat al mustakin* or Straight Path. Here is one such example: "Righteous are those secure in their belief in God, the hereafter, the angels, the scripture and the prophets; who give wealth lovingly for the love of God to relatives, orphans, the poor, travelers, petitioners, and who set slaves free; who keep the prayer and pay the zakat; who fulfill their promises when they make a promise, who are patiently constant during distress and affliction and in times of conflict. These are the truthful; these are the pious." (Quran 2:177)

## The five pillars

Belief alone is not enough to live a complete Islamic life. The Quran and *sunnah* emphasize practice—acting on the beliefs. Muslims believe that the quality of a person's actions determines the soul's place in the life to come. The Five Pillars of Islam are the structures of practice on which a Muslim's life is built. They frame the life of a Muslim from the call to perform the one-time pilgrimage (hajj) to guidance as to how to react in any given situation. The Five Pillars give Muslims the tools by which to exercise their beliefs and live a righteous and successful life.

### 1. Testimony of Faith (*shahada*)

This entrance into the Islamic faith is a testimony in two parts. Muslims bear witness, publicly and privately, in their intentions, words, and actions that there is no god but God and that Muhammad is a messenger of God.

In Arabic, the *shahada* sounds like this: *a-shadu a-la ilaha illallah, wa a-shadu anna Muhammad a-rasul-ullah.* One can hear it regularly on the lips of Muslims and during the call to prayer that rings out five times a day, spoken as a way of reminding themselves of God.

Declaring the *shahada* admits a person (of any background, culture, or religious tradition) into the Islamic faith. It is recorded in the hadith that Muhammad emphatically stated that any human being who says the *shahada* must have his or her life and property protected by the Muslim community (the *ummah*).

The goal of every Muslim is to live out the *shahada* in one's thoughts, words, and actions. The first part of the *shahada* states there is no god but God. On first glance, this sentence means that there is only God. God is unequaled and has no associate gods. Probing a little deeper, this sentence means that human beings are not to set up any rivals to God—things, ideas, or desires that take priority or precedence. Upon deeper investigation, still more meanings unfold. Some scholars translate this first part of the *shahada* to mean that there is no reality save an overarching spiritual reality. This viewpoint would mean that nothing in this earthly world is real in its own right; no thing generates its own energy. Nothing has any lasting power or strength; everything will at one time die, collapse, crumble, or disappear. Everything that exists does so for the duration that God allows it to continue to exist.

To Muslims, then, building a life based on flimsy material objects, and even on human relationships, is like building a house on quicksand. The material objects will crumble, and individuals will eventually die and be separated from those people and things they love. Muslims aim instead to build a life based on the bedrock of a divine reality, choosing to believe—even if they do not have any direct material or tangible proof—that the only real life is the life to come. This is a difficult concept for many people to accept, a point raised several times in the Quran when God laments people's inability to have faith in something they cannot see or fully comprehend.

Muslims view human existence in four stages: the womb, the life of this world, the grave, and the afterlife. Each soul moves through the successive stages. Just like the baby in the womb has no clue of what life outside the womb will be like, we have no idea what the experience of life in the grave will be like.

If, in the Islamic view, the worldly realm is a fleeting one, what then is the purpose of this life? Muslims believe that this world is an important testing ground to determine where a person will go in the next life. Every situation encountered, every human relationship developed is either an opportunity to do good or a hole into which a person may fall by doing wrong. The world is a place to accrue merit that will bear fruit in the afterlife, although Muslims do enjoy the good and *halal* things in life because God created them for human use and enjoyment.

The second part of the *shahada*—Muhammad is a messenger of God—is important in its relationship to the first part. Muhammad's life is a manifestation of God's message to humanity on how to live a good life. Muslims see the *sunnah* of Muhammad as both a responsibility and a liberation.

How is it a responsibility? With Muhammad's life and character as an example, Muslims believe there is no excuse to act in ways in which he would not have. Muslims look toward the actions and behavior of Muhammad for guidance on how to act in all situations.

Muslims see the second part of the *shahada* as a liberation and a mercy in that God did not send Muslims only the Quran to teach them how to live. He also sent a living example to learn from. The Quran and the *sunnah* set the parameters of the Straight Path (*sirat al mustakin*) that Muslims attempt to follow throughout their lives. But blind imitation (*taqlid*) is not encouraged in Islam. Rather, the Quran and the teachings of Muhammad emphasize the use of human reason: "Say (Oh Muhammad): This is my way: resting upon conscious insight, accessible to reason, I am calling you all to God—I and they who follow me." (Quran 12:108)

## 2. Five Daily Prayers (*salaat*)

Muslims believe that the human soul is a wisp of God's divine breath, that each individual soul came from him and will return to him. The Quran describes an agreement between human beings and God. Before being born, each human soul is asked to bear witness before God. He asks, "Am I not your Lord?" (Quran 7:172) All souls testify that indeed God is Lord. Yet often people get caught up in their daily lives and come to believe that this world is the only existence. If they do remember that there is more than material existence, it is a vague sense that comes in inspired moments.

Muslim mystics speak of veils existing between the individual and God. For Muslims, the ultimate task is to try to remove those veils to become conscious, albeit while in this earthly realm, of the truths of the other, higher realm—to strive to be as aware as possible of the divine presence at all times. The five daily prayers, which interrupt worldly life, encourage human beings to pause, remember, and become aware of God's presence.

There are two types of Islamic prayer. The formal, ritual prayer is called *salaat*. Personal communication with God, the second type of prayer, is called *du'a*, which means "supplication." *Salaat* is obligatory, whereas *du'a* is optional.

Muslims are required to offer *salaat* five times a day. First, a Muslim must purify him or herself by performing *wad'u*, or ablution, which entails running water over the hands, face, head, ears, nose, mouth, the arms up to the elbows, and the feet. Then the Muslim stands on a prayer mat, facing the direction of Mecca, and sets his or her intention to pray for the glorification of God.

During one cycle of prayer, or one *rakka*, a person begins standing, then bows forward, goes into full prostration, and ends in a seated position. Each movement is accompanied by the recitation of specific prayers, verses of the Quran, and magnifications of God. A person begins by reciting the first verse of the Quran followed by another verse of his or her choosing. The first verse of the Quran, called the Fatihah or Opening, can be translated as follows:

With curved and upturned hands,
a prayer is offered up.

**In the name of the merciful, compassionate God**
**All praise is for God, Lord of the worlds**
**The merciful, the compassionate**
**King of Judgment Day**
**You alone do we worship, and you alone do we turn to for help**
**Guide us along the straight path, the path of those whom you have blessed,**
**Not the path of those upon whom is your wrath, nor of those who have gone astray.**
**Amen. (Quran 1:1–7)**

The Fatihah is simultaneously a glorification of God, a plea for guidance, and an acknowledgment of submission. It is also called the Mother of the Book or the Foundation of the Quran in that it sums up the essential message of the Quran. A Muslim recites this verse at least seventeen times a day during the five daily prayers. The Muslim prayer ends by invoking God's blessings on Abraham and Muhammad.

Muslims believe that the angel Gabriel showed Muhammad how to perform the ritual ablution and the sequence of daily *salaat* when he revealed the Quran to him in the cave above Mecca. A few years later, during the Night Journey, as Muhammad passed through the levels of heaven he saw angels prostrating themselves to God in adoration, just as Gabriel had taught him. These same movements make up the ritual *salaat*. No matter the cultural or language differences among Muslims from Africa, Europe, Asia, or the Americas, when they meet one another in Mecca and stand side by side, they perform the same prayers in the same manner and in the same language, Arabic.

It was also during his Night Journey that God gave Muhammad the number of *salaat* a Muslim must pray each day. After his meeting with God, Muhammad started his descent through the heavens toward earth. On the way, he passed Moses who asked him the number of prayers that God had given to his people. "Fifty," Muhammad replied. Moses said, "Prayer is a weighty thing and your people are weak. Go back to God and ask him to reduce the number." So Muhammad went back, and God decreased the number. Again Moses insisted that this was too many for Muhammad's people. So he went back again and again until the number had been reduced to five. At that point he was ashamed to ask for further reductions. Thus, Muslims pray five times a day.

Each time of day requires a different number of *rakkats*. Muslims are obliged to pray two *rakkats* at dawn, four just after the sun reaches its zenith, four in the mid-afternoon, three at sunset, and four when night has fallen. The reason behind the number of *rakkats* at each time of day is mysterious—there is no clear or historical answer. But Abu Hamid al-Ghazālī (1058–1111), an Islamic intellectual who lived and taught in present-day Iraq, offered an interesting analysis: "Just as medicaments are composed of mixtures of elements differing in kind and quantity . . . likewise, the acts of worship, which are the remedies for the [maladies of the] heart, are composed of actions differing in kind and quantity so that a prostration is the double of a bowing, and the morning prayer is half as long as the afternoon prayer . . ."

Like a sick person following the advice of a qualified physician, following the spiritual prescriptions of the prophets can cure spiritual maladies. Al-Ghazālī identifies these maladies as including hypocrisy, egotism, and self-delusion. The benefits of following the prayer prescriptions are interior knowledge and awareness of God, which cures all spiritual maladies. Al-Ghazālī notes that all aspects of the spiritual prescription work cooperatively and synergistically. To get the best results, a patient does not mix medications. Rather he or she follows the course of one to completion. Thus, the *rakkats* of one particular time of day are complementary with the number of *rakkats* at other times of the day.

# the call to prayer

The Islamic call to prayer, the *adhan*, can be translated as follows:

> *God is most great. God is most great.*
> *I testify that there is no god except God.*
> *I testify that there is no god except God.*
> *I testify that Muhammad is the messenger of God.*
> *I testify that Muhammad is the messenger of God.*
> *Come to prayer! Come to prayer!*
> *Come to success (in this life and the hereafter)! Come to success!*
> *God is most great. God is most great.*
> *There is no god except God.*

The story behind the origin of the call to prayer can be traced to the early days of the Muslim community in Medina. As Muhammad was considering how to call the people to prayer—whether to use a bell, horn, or wooden clapper to summon the faithful—one of his followers came to him to tell him of a dream he had recently had. The Muslim had dreamed that a man dressed in green robes passed by carrying a wooden clapper. The Muslim asked if he could buy the clapper. The man inquired why he needed it. The Muslim replied that it would be used to call people to prayer, whereupon the man in green replied, "I'll show you a better way to summon the faithful." He then said, "God is great, God is great! I testify that there is no god but the one true God. I testify that Muhammad is the messenger of God. Come to prayer! Come to the highest place! God is great! There is no god but the one true God!"

The Muslim related this dream to Muhammad, who recognized it as a true vision and accepted it. He then assigned Bilal, a freed African slave and one of the first Muslims, who had a powerful voice, to call the *adhan*. So, Bilal went to the highest house in the oasis of Medina every morning before daybreak and sat on the roof until he saw the first thread of dawn light. Then he rose and, with his magnificent voice, recited the *adhan*. Today, the same *adhan* can be heard five times a day the world over.

### 3. The Fast of Ramadan (*sawm*)

During the holy month of Ramadan (the ninth month of the Islamic calendar), Muslims abstain from eating, drinking, smoking, and sexual activity from sunrise to sunset. Engaging in behavior always considered negative, such as lying, gossiping and cheating, can also break a person's fast.

The fast of Ramadan, like the fasts of other spiritual traditions, is an exercise intended to purify the body and senses, increase spiritual awareness, and unify the religious community. A fasting person understands what his or her neighbor is going through, and they both feel what it might be like to be hungry. Fasting increases an individual's compassion and understanding. Fasting makes tangible the weak and feeble human nature and also the strength of self-determination and the profound depth of spirit.

While fasting, people watch their own behavior carefully, striving for perfection—even a lustful look or an impatient word can be sufficient to break a person's fast. Muhammad once said that a fasting person who does not guard his or her tongue or avoid negative actions gains little from their fast except hunger and thirst.

Ramadan is a time for studying the Quran, praying, inner reflection, spending time with family, and retreating from the demands of daily life. Abstaining from everyday activities encourages a person to assume or access a different level of awareness. Ramadan affords Muslims an opportunity to evaluate their priorities and gives them time to spend in quiet contemplation.

### 4. Purifying Dues (*zakat*)

Each Muslim must give away a minimum of 2.5 percent of his or her wealth each year—this includes income, inheritance, and jewelry. The amount of *zakat* is higher, closer to 20 percent, if a Muslim makes his or her income in fields such as mining for oil or gemstones. Either way, by performing this act, the income a Muslim earns from his or her job is purified and turned into an act of worship. The purpose of *zakat* is to spread and attempt to equalize the wealth of a society.

The importance of charitable generosity is asserted again and again in the Quran. Charitable giving, in the form of money, food, or material items, or even as kind words, a smile, or the intimate relations between husband and wife, is highly encouraged in Islam. Hoarding and taking financial advantage of other people is absolutely discouraged. Muhammad is known to have said, "Bringing about a just reconciliation between two parties is charity; helping a person mount his animal or load his baggage is charity; a good word is charity; removing obstacles in the street is a charity; smiling at people is charity." It is important to remember that *zakat* is not considered relief for the needy in the community. It is a religious obligation incumbent on every Muslim household.

**An Iraqi girl reads from the Quran on the first day of Ramadan. During this ninth month of the Islamic calendar, Muslims are expected to fast from sunrise to sunset.**

### 5. Pilgrimage to Mecca (hajj)

"Proclaim to all people the duty of pilgrimage: they will come on foot and on every kind of fast mount, coming from every faraway point on earth, so that they might experience much that shall be of benefit to them . . ." (Quran 22:27)

The fifth pillar of Islam is the pilgrimage to Mecca, called the hajj. The hajj is made over five days in Dhul-Hijjah (the twelfth month of the Islamic lunar calendar). Muslims are required to undertake this pilgrimage once in their lifetime—if they are physically and materially able to do so. Today this annual ritual of pilgrimage to Mecca draws more than two million people from all over the globe.

The Ka'bah, known as "God's house" or the "navel of the world," is a cube-shaped structure made of stone. One pure black stone is set into its eastern corner. Having once housed the idols of the pre-Islamic Arabs, today the Ka'bah is virtually empty inside. It is in the direction of this cube that Muslims bow in prayer five times a day. Mosques throughout the world are built oriented in its direction. The dead are buried and animals sacrificed with their faces turned toward the Ka'bah. Muslims believe that directly above the earthly Ka'bah there is a heavenly one that the angels circle, while directly above the angelic Ka'bah is the throne of God (al-Arsh al-Adhim). For the last 1,400 years, Muslims have directed their passion, devotion, yearning, and joy toward Mecca.

Tradition dates the pilgrimage ritual to the time of Abraham. The ritual itself consists of circumambulating the Ka'bah seven times, ascending the nearby hill of Mount Arafat, and camping on the plains below it. Abraham's willingness to sacrifice his son Isaac as commanded by God, is remembered by performing a sacrifice, usually of a sheep. Pilgrims travel seven times between the hillocks of Safa and Marwa near the Ka'bah as a re-enactment of Hagar's panicked flight between the same two hillocks when she searched for water for a thirsty, young Ishmael. During Muhammad's last pilgrimage in the year 632, he formalized the rituals for future generations. Today Muslims perform the pilgrimage rituals as he did then.

Before embarking on the hajj, pilgrims purify themselves by entering a state called *ihram*. They start by washing using unperfumed soap. Then the men wrap themselves in two pieces of unsewn white

The hajj, or pilgrimage to Mecca, is one of the Five Pillars. Here pilgrims ritually circumambulate or walk around the Ka'bah, the focal point of Mecca and Islam's holiest site.

cloth to symbolize the equality of all humans before God, and women cover themselves from head to toe with only their faces and hands exposed. They perform two cycles of prayer and pronounce their intention to perform the pilgrimage. Once in the state of *ihram*, pilgrims must not adorn themselves with any beautifying agents such as makeup or perfume. They must abstain from hunting, sexual relations, gossip, lying, and thieving to be considered in a pure state.

Muslim jurists classify the Meccan pilgrimage rites as rites of devotion rather than as rites of understanding. Each act has complex ritual, spiritual, and historical symbolism. God says in the Quran: "Unto every community we have appointed different ways of worship which they ought to observe . . ." (Quran 22:67). That God has commanded these rituals is reason enough for Muslims to do them with great passion.

The hajj is also a unique bonding experience, bringing the *ummah* together. Mecca has always been an important crossroads in the Islamic world. "For centuries, the pilgrimage used to be the annual Islamic convention before annual conventions became the norm. People from all over the world got to know each other, learned from each other, and exchanged ideas and products," American imam Feisal Abdul Rauf noted. "Even until recently, one would go on pilgrimage and perhaps acquire a fine Persian carpet from an Iranian pilgrim or frankincense from an Omani."

In the words of religious scholar Frithjof Schuon, "The pilgrimage is a prefiguration of the inward journey towards the Ka'bah of the heart and purifies the community, just as the circulation of the blood, passing through the heart, purifies the body."

Pilgrimage to Mecca often changes everything in the life of a Muslim. Some die there, some plan to die there; others reach an elevated state of spiritual consciousness; some men shave their heads and some women don the headscarf out of a desire to heighten their remembrance of God and the spiritual path on which they are traveling. To many, pilgrimage is the realization of a dream they have spent their whole life planning and saving for. They cram into buses and bounce for miles across the Arabian Peninsula, or they fly first class from far-flung destinations. But when they arrive, dressed in two pieces of unsewn white cloth and stripped of material adornments, they stand shoulder to shoulder, equal before God.

# four

# STRUCTURE

## The earth is a prayer Rug

*"The earth has been made for me and for my followers a place for praying. . . . Therefore pray wherever the time of a prayer is due."*
—hadith of Muhammad

One of Islam's defining features is that it contains no structure of religious hierarchy—like the clergy or papacy of Christianity or the caste system of Hinduism headed by Brahmin priests. Instead, each Muslim is responsible for his or her own spiritual evolution and will eventually stand alone before God. But Islam offers vital tools that help prepare and purify a person for that ultimate meeting.

Muslims believe that humans were created to adore and worship God and that the ultimate happiness is to be close to him. To live in a way that earns his pleasure forms the trajectory of a Muslim's life. Perfecting one's relationship with God includes perfecting one's relationships with others. Islam contains an inner spiritual dimension and an outer social dimension: a Muslim hones the spiritual principles during acts of private worship and puts them into practice during daily social life.

The most important relationships are those with a person's immediate family—parents, spouse, and children; a person's extended family; the Islamic community and its spiritual leaders; the global society at large; and the rest of the created world—animals, plants, and the physical environment. Each relationship is governed by a specific etiquette (*adab*), which has as its underlying goal the desire to please God by striving to attain the attributes of *ihsan* (virtuous excellence). The structure of Islamic life, as the Muslim believer moves toward God, involves the functioning of individuals in relation to themselves, to their families and community, to the global Muslim *ummah*, and to the rest of the created universe.

## Loving the Divine

Each individual is responsible for maintaining and deepening his or her relationship with God and for increasing the quality of his or her spiritual life, striving against those forces that stand in the way of faith and tarnish the soul and embracing those forces that cleanse and uplift it. This is the lifelong, moment-by-moment effort of each Muslim.

In Arabic, the word for struggle or striving is *jihad,* a term that is often too narrowly translated as "holy war." A famous saying of Muhammad regarding jihad comes from a time when he and his companions were returning from battle; he commented that they were returning from the lesser jihad to the greater one—to the jihad against the ego and other illnesses of the human heart. Imam Feisal Abdul Rauf described jihad as "the psychological war you wage within yourself to establish the kingdom of God in your behavior and build a lifestyle in keeping with God's dictates."

Some of the spiritual tools that assist in a person's ascension to a higher level of spiritual understanding are theoretical, while others are of a more practical nature.

## Engaging the Quran

Muslims believe that the best way to begin to part the veils said to stand between each person and God is to study God's message to humanity—the Quran. The Quran is to be primarily understood as a recitation and its rhythm can only be understood properly when it is recited in Arabic, the original language of its revelation. Proper recitation is known as *tarteel*, which perhaps can best be translated as "resonant or harmonious recitation." There are many styles of recitation, but none of them changes the essential meaning of the text.

The Quran is said to have several layers of meaning—some of which are so esoteric they will never be known to human beings—and each individual must develop a personal relationship with the Quran through reciting it and studying its meaning.

The first and most important source of interpretation of the Quran is the Quran itself. In many instances, the Quran introduces a concept, phrase, or verse and then explains it. The next best source of interpretation is Muhammad, whose life was a living commentary on the Quran.

Muslims also study the interpretations of various scholars over the ages. The interpretation of the Quran has become an elaborate science known as *tafsir*. The earliest written interpretations, still in use today, appeared around the end of the ninth century and were based on the commentary of the companions of Muhammad.

Non-Muslims often complain that the Quran is difficult to read and understand—Muslims sometimes feel this way too. Hamza Yusuf Hanson, an American convert to Islam, offers one explanation: "The Quran is not a linear narration. It's a book that is coming at you from every angle. It is speaking in the first person. Suddenly, it's in the second person, then it's in the third person. It's speaking about the nature of God. And suddenly it's talking about inheritance laws and what you do when somebody dies. . . . The Quran in its own pages describes itself as being similar to the stars at night. . . . It appears to you to be a jumbled group of lights, of heavenly orbs that really don't have any pattern. But if you begin to look close, and . . . begin

**Friday prayers at the Umm al-Qura Mosque in Baghdad, Iraq, find this father and son studying a passage in the Quran together. The life of Muhammad, the writings of various religious scholars, and the Quran itself are seen as the holy book's most important sources of interpretation.**

to really reflect, gradually, this order begins to emerge. And that is the experience with the Quran. The Quran initially presents itself as a disorderly array of lights. But as you begin to immerse yourself in this book, a deeper order begins to emerge."

## loving the beloved of god

Another way Muslims attempt to get closer to God is to study the example of Muhammad and apply it to their own lives. Muhammad's words, actions, and reactions were recorded in detail by his companions as well as by scribes assigned for the purpose. One scribe was a highly literate boy called Anas. The boy's parents originally sent him to work as Muhammad's personal servant. Anas's job became to note Muhammad's words and deeds, which they would then review together.

The complex process of collecting and ranking the authenticity of hadith (each hadith was given an indicator of the probability of its veracity) began in the ninth century and resulted in six major compilations of authenticated hadith and numerous lesser-known ones. Notable among these compilations are Al-Muslim's *Sahih* and Al-Bukhari's *Sahih* (*sahih* means "true" or "valid"). The two scholars, Al-Muslim and Al-Bukhari, were meticulous about ensuring that every hadith was authentic, and they did so by tracing each one to Muhammad (this process is called *isnad*, meaning "chain"). Al-Bukhari is said to have traveled across central Asia and the Middle East collecting more than six hundred thousand hadith, of which he accepted 2,762 as solidly authentic.

Today Muslims know details of Muhammad's life, such as which of the numerous varieties of dates were his favorite. If a Muslim needs clarification on a certain topic, he or she can go to one of the books of hadith and look up what Muhammad said or did in a similar situation.

## perfecting the acts of devotion

A major tool Muslims have to guide them on the path toward God is the Five Pillars. Muslims perfect these five acts of worship by seeking the deepest meaning of the *shahada*, perfecting the timing and choreography of the five daily prayers, meeting all the criteria of fasting during Ramadan, ensuring that the correct amount of *zakat* is given at the proper time, and striving to make the pilgrimage to Mecca.

Performing the Five Pillars, although they are the minimum requirements of anyone who considers him or herself to be a Muslim, holds the potential for immense spiritual understanding and growth.

Beyond the Five Pillars, a Muslim may perform optional, additional acts of worship—which Muhammad himself used to do—to endear him or herself to God. These include extra prayers, prayers said late at night, fasting, meditations on the Quran, and charity beyond the *zakat*. Additional acts of worship can include sessions of *dhikr* (or remembrance, where people chant the names of God), memorizing the Quran, and seizing opportunities to do random acts of kindness.

## Traveling the Islamic Road

Muslims believe that the fastest and most direct way to God is to follow the Islamic road known in Arabic as the *shariah*, which literally means "the way to a watering place." The watering place is God, and the path is composed of the laws derived from the Quran and the *sunnah* of Muhammad.

The basic intent of the *shariah* (also known as Islamic law) is to safeguard the interests of each person in this world and the next. Specifically, the *shariah* protects five things: life, sanity, religion, wealth (including property), and family. If any of these things are violated, *shariah* is absent and justice is not being done. Justice is a main theme of the Quran, and a Muslim is required by the laws of the Quran to strive toward justice in all areas of life.

The primary sources of the *shariah* are the Quran, the *sunnah*, *ijma* (consensus among the Islamic community), and *qiyas* (analogies drawn from the *sunnah* on modern circumstances not directly addressed in the Quran or *sunnah*). Two other considerations are public interest (what is best for the *ummah*) and custom (cultural elements of a particular society). While the Quran is timeless and eternal, *shariah* laws evolve over time and adapt to the particular circumstances of a given moment or place.

# when things go wrong: ıslamic transgressions

The guiding principle as to what is lawful and what is prohibited in Islam is derived from the concepts of beauty (*husn*) and ugliness (*qubh*). Muhammad said, "God is beautiful and likes beauty" and Muhammad himself did not like extremes. Islam is described as the religion of the middle path. Anything that is not expressly forbidden (*haram*) is considered permissible (*halal*). Thus, the list of things permitted greatly outnumbers the list of things prohibited.

There is also an emphasis in the Quran on God's forgiveness, as reflected in the following verse: "Those who avoid the truly grave sins and shameful deeds, even though they may sometimes stumble, behold, your Sustainer is abounding in forgiveness." (Quran 53:32)

The major sins or crimes in Islam, called *hudud*, include acts such as murder, consuming intoxicants, gambling, stealing, lying, disrespecting one's parents, committing suicide, practicing magic, and associating anything with God.

## loving your neighbor

Social life in Islam—from family relations to business transactions to jurisprudence and how laws are organized—falls under the umbrella of religion. To earn the pleasure of fellow creatures is to earn God's pleasure. A Muslim's inner spiritual life manifests in his or her reactions to and interactions with the outer world. Society is a place where a Muslim puts into practice the lessons learned in the deepest recesses of the soul.

There are various elements of Islamic social life, starting with the most basic etiquette.

## Islamic Etiquette (adab)

Islamic morals and manners, *adab*, exist for every aspect of life—eating, drinking, speaking, washing, sleeping, waking, dressing, having sexual relations, working, studying, being a parent, being a child, being a friend, and being a member of the community—to name a few. Muslims believe that Muhammad had perfected his *adab*.

The *adab* of daily life is of the utmost importance in a Muslim's life and works in conjunction with

This woman walks past the ramparts that surround the medina in the Moroccan town of Taroudannt. She wears a traditional garment often referred to as a *chador*. The veil that leaves the area around her eyes exposed is often referred to as a *nikab*.

the *adab* of worship and the overall purpose of Islam, which is to live a clean, harmonious life as an individual, family member, and participant in a society that is oriented to the worship of God.

The Quran emphasizes the good treatment of parents. Muhammad identified one's mother as being the most important person to care for and is reported to have said, "Paradise lies at the feet of the mother."

Muslim men are responsible for their immediate female relatives. All Muslims are encouraged to keep close ties with their blood relatives and to help them in any way that is required. When giving *zakat*, a Muslim looks to poor or needy relatives first, because he or she will be accountable for them on the Day of Judgment. The Quran makes special mention of taking care of sick people, weak people, old people, poor people, orphans, travelers, and newcomers to town. It is considered good *adab* to accept social invitations and to reciprocate.

## The caliphate of the Human Being

In Islamic theology, the core of every person's spiritual self is known as the abode of harmony or the viceregency. God states in the Quran that human beings are God's representatives (caliphs) responsible for applying and upholding his laws on earth.

Human life, then, is a sacred trust. In simply living, human beings have been given a major task and how each person lives up to this responsibility will be carefully noted. This means executing the Five Pillars, but going even further. Responsibilities that come with being human include worshipping the one who created everything; seeking truth and justice; caring for one's physical body, caring for others; showing mercy, respect, kindness, compassion, and love towards all creatures; spreading peace, concord, and harmony; caring for the earth; and preventing injustice and oppression. In summary, Muslims strive to reflect the qualities of God through both their inner selves and their outward actions.

Cultivating personal strengths and attributes—being the best person one can be—is an important aspect of the viceregency. Attaining knowledge, power, and wealth is encouraged in Islam because these attributes make a person more effective and serve humanity better than do ignorance, weakness, and poverty.

The Quran and hadith are full of references to seeking knowledge, such as the following hadith: "The superiority of a learned person over a mere worshipper is like the superiority of the full moon over all the stars." The Quran also says: "God grants wisdom to whom he wills; and whoever is granted wisdom has indeed been granted wealth abundant." (Quran 2:269)

There is a hadith that encourages people to correct wrongs with rights—it is a social obligation for Muslims. Muhammad said, "When you see an evil act, stop it with your hand. If you can't, then at least speak out against it with your tongue. If you can't, then at least dislike it with all your heart, and this is the weakest of faith." So, even if a person is powerless to intervene in any way, sending corrective thoughts in the direction of the situation is enough.

Keeping the public peace is important and is reflected in the ways that Muslims strive to cover their faults and mistakes as well as others'. Muslims believe that if a person covers the faults of another, God will cover that person's faults on the Day of Judgment. Thus, the good of the group is more important than the good of the individual. At times in Islamic history, Muslims have accepted less-than-ideal rulers for the sake of social unity.

Finally, as God's representatives on earth, humans must look and act the part, even on the most seemingly superficial levels. In Islam, there are detailed requirements for personal hygiene and general upkeep, such as wearing clean and presentable clothes and trimming nails and hair. There are specific ways to wash before prayer, before embarking on pilgrimage, as well as after sexual relations, a menstrual period, and childbirth. Muhammad was fastidious about personal cleanliness and regularly kept his mouth fresh by chewing *miswak*, a stick known for its antiseptic qualities. He also loved perfume. Although men in the Muslim world are discouraged from wearing silk and gold, luxurious material symbols, they do keep themselves tidy and looking and smelling good. Women observe the same hygiene etiquette as men and beautify themselves with additional adornments, but the Quran instructs them to keep their beauty, both natural and embellished, concealed from the eyes of the general public.

# islamic Holidays

### Friday (Yawm al-Jummah)

Friday is called the Day of Gathering (Yawm al-Jummah), and every able-bodied man is required to attend the congregational noon prayer at a mosque. It is considered a mini-pilgrimage and a good bonding experience for the community. In most places, women can also attend and often do. Certain wealthy Gulf countries such as Oman and Qatar have beautiful large spaces for women to pray, air-conditioned and scented with the favorite incense of the region, *oud,* a wood from the tropical forests of Asia. On Fridays, people take a ritual shower, don their best clothing, apply perfume, and go to the mosque where the imam leads a sermon after which everyone prays. Businesses are shut from Thursday night through sunset on Friday for Yawm al-Jummah.

### Festival of Breaking the Fast (Eid al-Fitr)

Eid al-Fitr takes place at the end of Ramadan, the month of fasting. This festival begins with a congregational prayer in the morning. Then families and friends exchange visits over the next three days, dressed in their finest clothes. Children delight in outings, such as pony rides in public parks, and in exchanging gifts.

### Festival of Sacrifice (Eid al-Adha)

Eid al-Adha follows the pilgrimage to Mecca and is celebrated by all Muslims—not only those who embarked on the pilgrimage. This festival also begins with a congregational prayer followed by the sacrifice of an animal, symbolizing Abraham's willingness to sacrifice his son after receiving the command from God to do so. A third of the sacrificial meat is kept by the family who sacrificed the animal, a third is given to friends and family, and a third is given to the poor. The meat is received with joy and often cooked and eaten immediately.

**These men attend prayers for Eid al-Adha, a festival that commemorates Abraham offering his son as a sacrifice after a command from God.**

## A place of prostration

The mosque plays a central role in Islamic social life. Men are encouraged to pray the five daily prayers in communion with other Muslims at the mosque. On Fridays, men and women congregate there for the noon prayer and sermon. The mosque is also a center for social services. Money, food, and clothing are distributed to the poor; and children and adults come to learn the Quran and other Islamic studies.

The word *mosque* comes from the Arabic *masjid*, meaning place of prostrations. In pre-Islamic times, the area around the Ka'bah was called the *masjid*. Although Abu Bakr built a place of prayer next to his house in Mecca, the first mosque is considered to be the mosque Muhammad built in Quba near Medina where he stopped on the *hijrah*. Muhammad built the second mosque in Medina and used it for the rest of his life for prayer and sermons.

## Islam splintered

During Muhammad's lifetime, the Islamic community was one. But by the end of rule of the fourth caliph, Ali, the cousin of Muhammad, the first major ideological cracks had appeared within the *ummah*.

Some Muslims believed that Muhammad's successor should be a relative. These people came to be known as Shiites. The word *Shiite* can be defined as "followers, adherents, disciples, faction, party, sect." Shiites believe that Muhammad had designated Ali as his successor. Although none of Ali's offspring assumed the political position of caliph, they did hold the successive position of spiritual leader (imam) to the Shiite community. Today many Shiite imams trace their lineage back to Ali. Shiite Muslims account for about 15 percent of the more than one billion Muslims worldwide.

The other major group of Muslims believed that Muhammad's successor should be the most able person in the community, not necessarily a relative. They are known as Sunni Muslims, a reference to their dedication to the *sunnah* of Muhammad. Today, the majority of Muslims are Sunnis. Sunnis make up about 85 percent of the Muslim population.

In investigating the sects of Islam, the most important thing to remember is that belief in one God and in the prophethood of Muhammad is what makes a person a Muslim. Many Muslims today lament the fracture of the *ummah* into sects and echo the words of the theologian and jurist Ibn Taymiyya (1263–1328): "The Prophet has said, 'The Muslim is brother of the Muslim . . .' How, then, can it be permitted to the community of Muhammad to divide itself into such diverse opinions that a man can join one group and hate another one simply on the basis of presumptions or personal caprices, without any proof coming from God? Unity is a sign of divine clemency, discord is a punishment of God."

## A word on the sufis

From the earliest days of Islam, certain people were interested in an inward, esoteric orientation of the religion. These Muslims were called Sufis from the Arabic word *tasawwuf* (which comes from the word for "wool," as they often wore simple wool garments). Sufis are often called the "mystics of Islam" and are compared to the Cabalists of Judaism and the saints of Christianity. Sufis are primarily concerned with the essence of religion and their own spiritual development. That is not to say that they do not prescribe to the fundamental obligations of Islam. In fact, the opposite is often true: along with the ritual practices of the Islamic faith, Sufis perform additional, non-obligatory practices. They say extra prayers in the middle of the night, chant the names of God over and over, and recite certain verses of the Quran. Their purpose is to cleanse themselves of human ills such as anger, jealousy, arrogance, and excessive

**An Egyptian Sufi dancer whirls to the beat of percussion instruments on the eve of Muhammad's birthday.**

egotism and to create an increasing awareness of the divine presence. Sufis cultivate intense feelings of love in their hearts for God, and the Sufi path is often called the "path of love."

Some of the greatest thinkers in Islamic scholarship have been Sufis. Among them is Abu Hamid al-Ghazālī, who lived in modern day Iraq in the late 1000s and left a career as a university professor to travel through the Islamic world to seek knowledge. The Andalusian mystic Ibn al-'Arabī was a prolific thinker and writer who died in Damascus in 1240. And today, one of the most popular poets in the United States is the Sufi saint Jalāl ad-Dīn ar-Rūmī, who lived and taught in the 1200s in present-day Turkey.

Sufis have often been viewed with suspicion in the eyes of the rest of the *ummah* for their perceived unorthodox practices, except for a period of time between 1300 and 1800 when many Muslims were members of one or another Sufi order. Today, Sufis are active throughout the Muslim world, including Africa, Turkey, Bosnia, western Asia, and India. Sufi orders are also flourishing in the Western world, where non-Muslims find the loving Sufi approach to Islam very appealing.

# five

# THE *UMMAH* TODAY

*"We have created you all out of a male and a female and made you into nations and tribes so that you might come to know one another." (Quran 49:13)*

From the small community of Muslims struggling to survive persecution in the Arabian Desert 1,400 years ago, today Islam is the world's second-largest religion, after Christianity. More than one billion Muslims live in the world; one person in five defines him or herself as a Muslim. Today, about fifty countries have Muslim-majority populations. Some countries have a large albeit minority Muslim population, and nearly every country has some Muslims living within its borders.

Although many people view Islam as a cultural monolith, the Muslim world is, in reality, extremely diverse. Fewer than 15 percent of all Muslims are Arab, and most Muslims live in Asia. Indonesia has the largest Muslim population of any country.

Islam has come to be expressed through many different cultures, but the Five Pillars are practiced identically the world over. A congregation of Muslims praying the Friday prayer in Senegal goes through the same ritual motions as does a congregation in Bangladesh or the United States, and the language of prayer is universally Arabic. But the sermon may be delivered in different languages (Wolof, Bangladeshi, or English, for example); the people may wear different items (a *boubou*, a *salwar kameez*, or jeans and a T-shirt);

These young women in Senegal share a laugh after gathering for prayers marking Eid al-Adha at an outdoor mosque in the nation's capital, Dakar.

the architecture of the mosque may differ; and when the prayers are finished, the people return to their vastly different lives.

Likewise, many Islamic values and manners (*adab*) are consistent across borders. Strong family ties, based on the Quran's insistence on respectful treatment of parents and keeping good relations with relatives, are apparent across the Muslim world. Drinking alcohol is not common in observant Muslim communities, and where it does happen it is kept hidden from public view. A conservative attitude about the social mixing of men and women is another Islamic value.

Countries differ in their interpretations of the orthodox teachings of Islam. In Saudi Arabia, for example, prayer times are enforced with shops, restaurants, and businesses closing five times a day. As it is a traditional and conservative culture, women are not allowed to drive and most are completely covered from head to toe in black *abayas* (cloaks). On the Indian subcontinent, on the other hand, women wear colorful outfits and generally do not cover all of their hair. (Some may wear a scarf draped loosely over their head.) Women in the subcontinent not only drive but even take political office. Four Muslim-associated countries—Bangladesh, Pakistan, Turkey, and Indonesia—have seen women heads of state in recent years. There are constant discussions within the *ummah* over which practices are cultural and which are "Islamic."

The diversity of Muslims in the world today lends richness to the *ummah*. The mixing of people from the Islamic world and the West, as well as converts to the Islamic faith, is invigorating the Islamic experience, but it also adds a wealth of differences in opinion and interpretations. Nowhere is this more apparent than in the United States.

## islam in the united states
Not unlike the first Muslims who fled persecution in Mecca to live a better life in Medina, Muslims today flee repressive regimes in their

homelands or seek better education and opportunities in the West. Muslim emigrants from regions such as Palestine, Kashmir, and Bosnia find refuge on American soil.

It is difficult to gauge the precise number of Muslims living in the United States, but demographers put the number anywhere from two to six million. The largest number of Muslims in the United States are of south and central Asian heritage, followed by those of African American heritage, then by those of Arab heritage.

The Muslim American community is made up of three main groups. The first group includes immigrants from all countries of the Islamic world and their children. The children of these immigrants— the second or even third generations—are the ones who have bridged the gap between the worlds their parents came from and life in the United States. African Americans make up the second group. Americans who converted to Islam comprise the third and smallest group.

Ingrid Mattson, a professor of Islamic studies at the Hartford Seminary, identifies three different Muslim responses to mainstream American culture. There are those who resist and view American culture as being *jahili* (immoral and ignorant of Islam) and tend to isolate themselves in Islamic neighborhoods; those who embrace American culture and see it as being to varying degrees concordant with Islamic values; and those who selectively engage with mainstream American culture and effect social change while remaining highly conscious of the limits placed on them by their religion.

Muslims in the United States act as catalysts for change in the way Islam is practiced the world over. The rich combination of civil society and the general freedom of religious expression found in the United States offer fertile ground for the development of new ideas among Islamic thinkers, reformers, and intellectuals. Their intellectual contributions, in fields such as *fiqh*, creative endeavors in film, literature, and art, and in social progress have resonance throughout the Islamic world.

American Muslims are particularly enthusiastic in addressing the biggest question: What does it mean to be Muslim in the modern context? In all periods of its history, the Muslim *ummah* has had to define its understanding of itself in the particular circumstances of the day. Today, Muslims ponder how they are to apply a 1,400-year-old message to a modern context.

## A Look Back in Time . . .

The early history of Muslims in the United States is murky. Muslims came with the slave ships from Africa in the early 1600s. Many of the first-generation Africans maintained their Islamic identity, but this identity became weaker in succeeding generations as they were encouraged to convert to Christianity.

In the late 1800s and early 1900s, waves of immigrants, primarily from Syria, Lebanon, and Palestine, arrived in the United States to start new lives, They were mostly unskilled workers eager for the opportunities offered by the new land, and they succeeded through education and effort. They established communities in places such as Detroit, Michigan; Cedar Rapids, Iowa; Ross, North Dakota; and Pittsburgh, Pennsylvania.

In the 1920s and 1930s, the African American movement began to gain momentum as African Americans looked to Africa for inspiration. Many found Islam. Malcolm X, one of the most famous African American Muslim figures, joined the somewhat unorthodox Nation of Islam movement in the 1950s. But after returning from performing the hajj to Mecca in 1964, Malcolm X started to lead African American Muslims toward orthodox Islam. He was assassinated in 1965, but the movement he initiated became the American Muslim Mission, a large African American Islamic base that exists today.

The next wave of Muslims from the Middle East came after the demise of the Ottoman empire, at the end of World War I. Then, in the 1950s, another wave of Arab Muslims, mostly refugees and professionals frustrated with a lack of options in their own lands, arrived in the United States. Aiding the post–World War II immigration was the McCarran-Walter Act of 1952, which allowed a larger quota of Asian immigrants into the United States.

Large numbers of students started arriving around this time also. This was the dawn of the American Muslim intellectual movement. During this period, Muslim communities developed, mosques were built, and national Islamic groups, such as the Muslim Students Association and the Islamic Society of North America (ISNA), formed. Visiting scholars and the first missionary groups from the Islamic world won a small number of white American converts.

Today mosques and Islamic schools and centers can be found in almost every urban center in the United States. Muslims across the country hold elected positions as mayors, judges, city council members, and state representatives and Muslims are represented in nearly every profession. In large cities such as New York or Los Angeles, Muslims tend to frequent mosques based on ethnicity. South Asians tend to gather in particular mosques, while West Africans attend others, for example.

## september 11, 2001: a turning point

The events of September 11, 2001, had a huge impact on Muslims in the United States. After the attacks, the American landscape changed for many American Muslims as they found themselves facing new questions and new challenges. Latent prejudice against Arabs and Muslims surfaced and often resulted in hostile and sometimes violent encounters. Some Muslims from various countries, who had lived in the United States for long periods of time, were forced to register with the government, causing them hardship and humiliation. Others were detained or even deported, some without apparent reason.

**A young businesswoman, clad in her *hijab*, uses her laptop computer.**

Some Muslims tried to blend into society—women who normally wore the headscarf took it off, for example. Others felt a need to speak out against the attacks, quoting passages from the Quran that forbid suicide and violence and highlight peace.

The majority of American Muslims expressed sorrow over the attacks as well as shock and betrayal that such an act could be associated with Muslims. After the attacks of September 11, 2001, many moderate Muslims realized that extremists were increasingly usurping the intellectual and political space—not only within Muslim states but also within the Muslim world.

Around this time, a new genre of popular Muslim preacher started drawing the attention of young Muslims around the world. According to an article by Asef Bayat in the Egyptian *Al-Ahram Weekly,* "The convergence of youth sub-culture, elitism, and a pietistic Islam have

# the headscarf

*Hijab* literally means "partition" and commonly refers to the headscarf worn by many Muslim women. Modesty is an Islamic prescription and one point of *hijab* is modesty; another is to identify a woman as being a Muslim. But the issue is surrounded by various questions debated by Muslims and non-Muslims, men and women, alike.

Some Muslim scholars believe that *hijab* is absolutely mandatory and interpret the verses in the Quran on the topic to mean that the only parts of a woman decent to be revealed in public are her hands, feet, and face. (24:31) They refer to another verse that says Muslim women should draw their outer garments over themselves in public to be distinguished as decent, believing women. (33:59) These scholars also point to many hadith that deal with the subject.

Other scholars say that *hijab* was a custom of the time period of Muhammad and open to change with the times. They add that all high-class women of that era, even in non-Muslim lands, covered their hair to protect their stature and dignity. Another issue surrounding *hijab* is whether or not it liberates or oppresses women. Opponents of *hijab* point to the fact that some women forego wearing it altogether, seeing it as blurring or obliterating their individuality and visibility. Other women do not choose to wear it themselves and are either directly forced to wear it by their husbands and families or the laws of the land, or feel indirectly compelled by the pressures of a conservative society to protect their reputation. Some women, however, do not see any link between oppression and *hijab*—they see the opposite. Many report being treated with greater respect and dignity while wearing the *hijab*. They face the hardships encountered by wearing the garment (such as judgments by others or difficulties in playing certain sports) with the inner conviction that they are earning God's pleasure. For many Muslim women, their *hijab* reminds them of their spiritual path and allows them to deepen their spiritual practice by renouncing certain worldly vanities.

come together to produce this new genre" thick in Islamic ritual and thin on politics, and currently being described as the "phenomenon of Amr Khaled." Egyptian-born Amr Khaled is a former accountant and gifted speaker who captivates audiences as he calls them to practice true Islam, to be proactive in contributing to their communities, to give to the poor, to vote in elections, and not to smoke, litter, or be lazy. Millions of young Muslims are responding with vigor to his call, which he communicates through satellite television and the Internet (in Arabic, English, French, German, and Italian).

The attacks of September 11, 2001, prompted Muslims to take a closer look at their identity as Americans, Muslims, and both. Many found themselves in a polarized position, feeling loyalty to both the United States and the Muslim world. As material and information about Islam poured into bookstores and newsstands, and as debates raged around the world as to whether the attacks were Islamic or un-Islamic, American Muslims found themselves called on to represent the Muslim world to the United States and the United States to the Muslim world. Islam was suddenly in the mainstream, and American Muslims were the spokespeople. They were asked questions such as what it means to be a Muslim American and whether or not the United States is a country that upholds Islamic ideals.

## is the united states a *shariah*-compliant country?

Conservative Islamic circles have long viewed the United States with suspicion, partially due to the fact that the nation is not governed by Islamic law and partially due to its flourishing popular culture, which they see as immoral and contrary to the basic principles of Islam. American foreign policies toward nations in the Muslim world, both today and in the past, have contributed to the negative impressions.

But, although the United States does not govern itself by the *shariah,* many Muslims who live in the United States feel that they are actually living in one of the most Islamic countries in the world, in terms of obtaining the rights and freedoms they need to practice their religion. Many report feeling a greater sense of dignity, respect and freedom living in the United States than in any other country.

Imam Hamza Yusuf, an American convert to Islam who founded the Zaytuna Institute, an Islamic institute in California, and is popular among young Muslims the world over, said, "I would rather live as a Muslim in the West than in most of the Muslim countries, because I think the way Muslims are allowed to live in the West is closer to the Muslim way. A lot of Muslim immigrants feel the same way, which is why they are here."

Some Muslim scholars maintain that the U.S. Constitution protects all the aspects of human life that Islam's *shariah* aims to guard (life, liberty, and the pursuit of happiness) and implements the Islamic concept of pluralism in matters of gender, race, national origin, and religion.

As Imam Feisal Abdul Rauf noted, "Many Muslims regard the form of government that the American founders established a little over two centuries ago as the form of governance that best expresses Islam's original values and principles."

These views may surprise those Muslims and non-Muslims who like to point out the divergence rather than the convergences of values between Islam and the United States. But American Muslims have noted the harmony struck between the values of their religion and the values of the modern, secular, and pluralistic American context. Younger Muslims, in particular, have selected and combined elements from both their Islamic background and current American context. Many of these individuals are excelling in their studies and professions; they are founding organizations and institutes to help new Muslim immigrants adapt to the American scene or to contribute to causes in the Muslim world. They are educating themselves on the finer points of Islamic jurisprudence, tackling the Arabic of the Quran, and becoming leaders in their own communities. They are bringing the Islamic experience into the American mainstream and enlivening the timeless message of Muhammad.

# TIME LINE

570
Muhammad is born in Mecca.

595
Muhammad marries Khadijah, a wealthy businesswoman fifteen years his senior.

608
The rebuilding of the Ka'bah. Muhammad resolves conflict between the tribes and secures his reputation as al-Amin, the trustworthy.

610
Muhammad receives the first verses of the Quran and shares them with his family members.

613
Muhammad begins to preach publicly.

615
The first Islamic migration: a small group of Muslims flees persecution in Mecca and takes refuge in Abyssinia.

620
Muhammad's Night Journey.

622

*Hijrah*. Muhammad and seventy Muslim families immigrate north to the oasis town of Yathrib, which becomes known as al-Medina al-Nabi (City of the Prophet).

623

Muhammad marries Aishah.

624

Battle of Badr. The Muslims defeat the Meccans. Jewish tribes begin to be exiled from Medina.

625

The Meccans retaliate in the battle of Uhud.

627

Battle of the Trench. Meccans attempt to attack Medina but cannot reach the city because the Muslims have dug a trench around the city. After the battle, Muhammad has the Jewish tribe of Qurayzah killed or sold as slaves for breaking its pact with him and supporting the Meccans against the Muslims.

628

Muhammad and a group of unarmed Muslims make a pilgrimage to Mecca. They do not reach Mecca, but instead sign a peace treaty with the Meccans on the plain of Hudaybiyah.

629

Muslims perform their first pilgrimage to Mecca; Bilal calls the prayer from the top of the Ka'bah.

630

Meccans breach the treaty of Hudaybiyah and the Muslims take Mecca; Arabians side with Muhammad. The Ka'bah is cleared of idols.

**632**

Muhammad gives his last sermon at Arafat. He dies in the arms of Aishah and is buried in her room. Abu Bakr becomes caliph.

**633**

Arabia is united.

**634**

Abu Bakr dies; Umar is elected caliph.

**635**

Conquest of Syria, beginning a series of Muslim conquests in Asia Minor.

**637**

Umar establishes the Islamic lunar calendar beginning with the year of the *hijrah*. Muslims conquer Jerusalem.

**640**

Conquest of Egypt.

**644**

Umar is assassinated by a Persian prisoner-of-war. Uthman assumes the caliphate.

**650**

The Quran is collated into one volume.

**656**

Uthman is assassinated in Medina by Arab soldiers. Ali becomes caliph.

**661**

Ali is assassinated. Muawiyyah becomes caliph. The Umayyad dynasty begins.

**667**

Arab armies reach central Asia.

670

Ali's son, Hasan, dies. Muslim armies cross North Africa and reach the Atlantic Ocean.

678

Aishah dies.

680

Hussain, Ali's second son, is killed in Iraq.

691

The Dome of the Rock and al-Aqsa mosque are built in Jerusalem.

711

Arabs enter Spain.

732

Muslim advance into France is checked by Charles Martel.

750

The Abbasid dynasty is founded.

756

Abd al-Rahman founds a dynasty in Cordoba, Spain.

935

The Abbasid caliphate is reduced to symbolic authority.

969

Shiite Fatimid rule is established in northern Africa.

973

Al-Azhar Mosque is dedicated in Cairo.

990–1118

The Seljuk empire, composed of nomadic converts to Islam from central Asia, is established.

1099
Crusaders conquer Jerusalem.

1187
Salah al-Din defeats the Crusaders and takes back Jerusalem.

1220-1231

The Mongols arrive from central Asia.

1225
Muslim rule in Spain dwindles to the small kingdom of Granada.

1250
The Mamluks establish a dynasty in Egypt and Syria.

1258
The Abbasid caliphate ends. Mongols sack Baghdad.

1256–1335
A branch of Mongols rules Iraq and Iran.

1369–1405
Timurlane, a Mongol, conquers much of Asia Minor (Turkey), the Middle East, and northern India.

1453
Mehmet II conquers Constantinople. It becomes the capital of the Ottoman empire.

1492
Catholic monarchs Ferdinand and Isabella take Granada from the Muslims.

1502–1524
Safavid empire rises to power in Iran.

1517
Ottomans conquer Egypt and Syria, ending the Mamluk rule.

1520–1566
Suleiman the Magnificent expands the Ottoman empire, which reaches its peak.

1560–1605
Mughal empire in India reaches the height of its power under Akbar.

1632–1649
Shah Jahan constructs the Taj Mahal in Agra, India.

1658-1707
Last major Mughal emperor, Aurangzeb, rules India.

1774
Russians defeats the Ottomans in the first Russo-Turkish War.

1798–1801
Napoleon occupies Egypt.

1803–1813
The Al-Sa'ud family, with the support of the Wahabbis, take the Hijaz, in modern-day western Saudi Arabia, from Ottoman control.

1830
France occupies Algeria.

1854–1856
England, France, and the Ottoman empire fight Russia in the Crimean War.

1857–1858
Indian mutiny against British rule in India.

1860
France takes control of Lebanon as an autonomous province and installs a French governor.

1901
Abd al Aziz Ibn Sa'ud takes the Arabian city of Riyadh. France invades Morocco. Oil concessions in Iran are granted to the British.

1914–1918
World War I. Egypt is declared a British protectorate; Iran is occupied by British and Russian troops.

1916
Arabs are allied with the British in a revolt against the Ottoman empire.

1917
The Balfour Declaration gives British support to the creation of a Jewish homeland in Palestine.

1920
The provinces of the Ottoman empire are divided between the British and French, who establish protectorates and mandates.

1921
Reza Khan founds the Pahlavi dynasty in Iran.

1923
Ataturk sets up an independent Turkish state.

1932
The Kingdom of Saudi Arabia is formed.

1928
Hassan al Banna founds the Muslim Brotherhood in Egypt.

1945
Turkey joins the United Nations. The Arab League is formed.

1947
India is divided into Hindu India and Muslim Pakistan.

1948
The Jewish state of Israel is created as a result of a UN declaration.

1952
Jamal Abd al-Nasser takes power in Egypt.

1965
Malcolm X is assassinated.

1967
Six-day War between Israel and Egypt, Jordan, and Syria.

1969
Twenty-five states join the Organization of the Islamic Conference.

1978
Anwar al-Sadat of Egypt signs the Camp David peace initiative with Israel.

1979
Iranian Revolution; Ayatollah Khomeini becomes the leader of the Islamic Republic of Iran.

1980
Iran-Iraq War begins.

1981
Islamic extremists kill Egyptian president Anwar al-Sadat.

1987
Beginning of the First Intifada, or Palestinian uprising, against Israel.

1988
UN cease-fire plan ends the Iran-Iraq War.

1990
Saddam Hussain invades and annexes Kuwait. Chechnya calls for sovereignty.

**1991**
United States–led coalition forces launch Operation Desert Storm against Iraq, and Iraq gives up Kuwait.

**1992**
Bosnia and Herzogovina declare independence; Bosnian Serbs declare a separate state.

**1993**
Israel and the Palestinian Liberation Organization (PLO) agree to autonomy for the Gaza Strip and Jericho in the Oslo Accords.

**1995**
Yizhak Rabin is assassinated by an Israeli extremist for signing the Oslo Accords.

**1996**
The Taliban captures Kabul, Afghanistan.

**1999**
General Pervez Musharraf stages a coup in Pakistan.

**2000**
The Second Intifada begins after Israeli politician Ariel Sharon visits the Dome of the Rock in Jerusalem.

**2001**
Nineteen extremists hijack four American passenger planes and crash them into the World Trade Center, the Pentagon in Washington D.C., and a field in Pennsylvania. As a result, the U.S. government begins its War on Terror.

**2003**
The U.S. military enters Iraq.

**2005**
The Islamic Conference holds summit in Mecca.

# GLOSSARY

*adab*—Islamic rules of conduct, discipline, and manners in accordance with the *sunnah*, or ways of the Prophet Muhammad. There is specific etiquette for every aspect of life, including business transactions, home life, familial relationships, intimate relationships, and acts of worship.

**Aisha**—The youngest and favorite wife of Muhammad. Intelligent, observant, and devoted, Aisha is the source of many hadith. She participated in battles after Muhammad's death and was the only woman in whose presence he received revelations. Aisha obtained the title Mother of the Believers, and died in Medina in 678 at the age sixty-seven.

**Al-Azhar**—A mosque and one of the oldest and largest centers of Islamic learning, located in Cairo, built in 969 shortly after the founding of Cairo.

**caliph**—A successor, viceregent, or deputy to Muhammad who was vested with authority in all matters of state, both civil and religious.

*dhikr*—Also *zikhr*; the practice of remembering God through the recitation of his names.

*du'a*—Prayer in the form of supplication (personalized, private prayer) as opposed to *salat*, which is prayer in the liturgical form. Performing *du'a* is a non-obligatory practice that Muslims generally add to the end of each *salat*.

**fard**—A religious obligation as spelled out in the Quran. The five-times-a-day prayer, for example, is a *fard*.

**Fatima**—A daughter of Muhammad by his first wife Khadijah. She married Ali, a cousin of Muhammad, and gave birth to Hasan and Hussain. Set apart from the other women of her time by her strong character, Fatima is often referred to as *Fatima az-zahra* (Fatima the resplendent). Muhammad called her one of the four exemplary women of history.

**fatwa**—A formal legal opinion or decision pronounced by an Islamic jurist or recognized religious authority.

**fiqh**—Understanding or jurisprudence. *Fiqh* is the science that deals with applying Islamic law (*shariah*), as derived from the Quran, hadith, and the *sunnah* of Muhammad, to real life issues.

**Five Pillars**—The five duties of Islam, which are to testify that there is no god but God and that Muhammad is the last messenger of God; observe the five daily prayers; fast during the month of Ramadan; give alms; and make the pilgrimage to Mecca.

**hadith**—Plural *ahadith*; a report or tradition, usually relating the behavior, words, or actions of Muhammad but also regarding the actions of his companions or other early authorities.

**hajj**—The pilgrimage to Mecca performed during the twelfth month of the Islamic calendar year. It is the fifth pillar of Islam.

**hanif**—Plural *hunafa*; in the Quran, a person who adheres to monotheism. Before the advent of Muhammad, most Arabs were not *hunafa*, rather, they worshipped a plurality of gods.

**hijrah**—Meaning "migration," the word has four meanings: the departure of Muhammad from Mecca to Medina; the Muslim calendar; the act of a Muslim leaving a country under non-Muslim rule; fleeing from sin.

**ihsan**—A state of being that connotes excellence or virtue in every action a person performs.

**ijma**—Consensus of opinion on a question of Islamic law. Along with the Quran, hadith, and *sunnah, ijma* legitimizes law.

**iman**—Faith. The sincere belief of the heart and declaration of the lips to the existence of God, angels, prophets, messages of the prophets, and the Day of Judgment.

**islam**—Surrender to the will of God.

**jahiliyyah**—Ignorant or untaught. *Jahiliyyah* refers to the period of paganism and ignorance before the revelation of Islam to Muhammad.

**jihad**—A holy struggle or war. Jihad also refers to the psychological war a person wages within.

**Ka'bah**—Meaning "cube"; the cube-shaped building in the center of the mosque at Mecca; it is considered the first house constructed for the worship of one God.

**kafir**—Plural *kafirun;* an atheist, a nonbeliever; a person or people within any faith or cultural tradition who reject the existence of God.

**Khadijah**—The first wife of Muhammad.

**Medina**—Meaning "the city" or "the city of the prophet." A city 200 miles northeast of Mecca, known as Yathrib before Muhammad and the early community of Muslims took refuge there after fleeing Mecca.

**Mecca**—The birthplace of Muhammad and the site of the Ka'bah. The city lies 70 miles inland from the Red Sea, in a sandy valley running north-south. It was the seat of government during the rule of the first five caliphs.

**Muslim**—A person who has submitted to God's will, from the root word *aslama*, meaing "to surrender" or "to seek peace."

*sajdah*—Prostration; the act of worship whereby the person's forehead touches the ground in prostration.

*salaat*—The formal, liturgical form of prayer, which believers are required to perform five times a day.

*sawm*—To fast.

*shahada*—The testimony of faith, bearing witness to the fact that there is no reality but God and that Muhammad is the messenger of God; the first pillar of belief in Islam.

*sira*—The life story of Muhammad.

**Shiite**—A member of the branch of Islam who regards Ali and his descendants as the legitimate successors to Muhammad and who rejects the first three caliphs.

*shura*—Consultation among adult Muslims on questions of rule of law.

*shariah*—Often translated as Islamic law, but more accurately, the *shariah* is a set of values, laws, and ethics derived from the Quran.

**Sufism**—Popularly called the mystical branch of Islam, Sufism is the journey of the human consciousness toward divine consciousness, from the absence of awareness of God to a state in which there is a maximal presence with God.

**sunnah**—Meaning "trodden path," precedent, local custom, or traditional practice. The jurists have defined the *sunnah* of Muhammad to mean everything he did or said.

**Sunni**—The branch of Islam that accepts the first four caliphs as rightful successors of Muhammad.

**tafsir**—Meaning "explaining." A term used for any commentary on a text but particularly refers to commentary on the Quran.

**taqlid**—Imitation in matters of law; following the opinions of others, sometimes with the connotation that one follows without understanding or scrutiny; accepting the rulings of others when such rulings are not coupled with a conclusive argument.

**ulema**—A group of scholars or a learned people; from the root word *ilm*, or "knowledge." The singular is *alim*.

**ummah**—The sum total of Muslims. The body-politic or nation of Islam. The *ummah* is not defined by ethnic, political, geographical, or social characteristics, but by religious orientation.

**zakat**—Meaning "purification." One of the Five Pillars of Islam. *Zakat* is a portion of a person's property given to help the needy.

# FURTHER RESOURCES

**BOOKS**

Abdul Rauf, Feisal. *What's Right with Islam: A New Vision for Muslims and the West.* San Francisco: HarperSan Francisco, 2004.

———. *Islam, A Sacred Law, What Every Muslim Should Know about the Shariah.* Brattleboro, VT: Qiblah Books, 1999.

Abou El Fadl, Khaled. *Islam and the Challenge of Democracy.* Princeton, NJ: Princeton University Press, 2004.

Abu Hamza, Al-Arabi. *Who Is Allah and His Prophet?* ed. Raymond J. Manderola. Riyadh, Saudi Arabia, and London: Darussalaam, 2001.

Ajami, Fouad. *The Dream Palace of the Arabs: A Generation's Odyssey.* New York: Vintage Books, 1999.

Arberry, A. J. *Aspects of Islamic Civilization: As Depicted in the Original Texts.* Ann Arbor: University of Michigan Press, 1964, 1971.

Armstrong, Karen. *Islam: A Short History.* New York: Modern Library, 2002.

———. *Muhammad: A Biography of the Prophet.* San Francisco: Harper San Francisco, 1992.

Arnold, Thomas. *The Spread of Islam in the World, A History of Peaceful Preaching.* London: Goodword Books, 2003.

Asad, Muhammad. *This Law of Ours and Other Essays.* Kuala Lampur, Malaysia: Islamic Book Trust, 2001.

———. *The Message of the Qu'ran.* Bristol, England: The Book Foundation, 2003.

———. *The Road to Mecca.* New York: Simon & Schuster, 1954.

Barks, Coleman and Michael Green. *The Illuminated Prayer: The Five-Times Prayer of the Sufis.* New York: Ballantine Wellspring, 2000.

Bloom, Jonathan and Sheila Blair. *Islam, Empire of Faith.* London: BBC, 2001.

Chittick, William C. *Sufism: A Short Introduction.* Oxford, England: Oneworld Publications, 2000.

Eaton, Gai. *Remembering God: Reflections on Islam.* Cambridge, England: Islamic Texts Society, 1994.

Fromkin, David. *A Peace to End all Peace: The Fall of the Ottoman Empire and the Creation of the Modern Middle East.* New York: Avon Books, 1990.

Ghazzālī. *Deliverance from Error.* Translated by Richard Joseph McCarthy. Louisville, KY: Fons Vitae, 1999.

Glassé, Cyril. *The New Encyclopedia of Islam.* Walnut Creek, CA: AltaMira Press, 2001.

Haddad, Yvonne Yazbeck and Adair T. Lummis. *Islamic Values in the United States.* New York: Oxford University Press, 1987.

Ibn al-Naqīb, Ahmad ibn Lu-lu. *Reliance of the Traveller: A Classic*

*Manual of Islamic Sacred Law.* Revised edition. Translated by Nuh Ha Mim Keller. Beltsville, MD: Amana Publications, 1999.

Ibrahim, Ezzeddin and Denys Johnson-Davies, translators. *Forty Hadith Qudsī.* Cambridge, England: Islamic Texts Society, 1997.

Islam, Yusuf. *The Life of the Last Prophet.* Chicago: Mountain of Light, 2001.

Jalāl al-Din Rumi, Maulana. *The Essential Rumi.* Translated by Coleman Barks, with John Moyne, A. A. Arberry, and Reynold Nicholson. San Francisco: Harper San Francisco, 1995.

———. *The Sufi Path of Love: The Spiritual Teachings of Rumi.* Translated by William C. Chittick. Albany, NY: State University of New York Press, 1983.

Khalidi, Tarif. *The Muslim Jesus, Sayings and Stories in Islamic Literature.* Cambridge, MA: Harvard University Press, 2001.

Khouj, Abdullah Muhammad. *Islam, Its Meaning, Objectives and Legislative System.* Washington, DC: The Islamic Center, 1994.

Kosmin, Barry A. and Seymour P. Lachman. *One Nation under God: Religion in Contemporary American Society.* New York: Harmony Books, 1993.

Lings, Martin. *Muhammad: His Life Based on the Earliest Sources.* Rochester, VT: Inner Traditions International, 1983.

Maqsood, Raqaiyyah Waris. *The Muslim Prayer Encyclopaedia, A Complete Guide to the Prayers As Taught by the Prophet Muhammad.* New Delhi, India: Goodword Books, 2002.

Mubarakpuri, Safiur-Rahman. *History of Madinah Munawwarah.* Translated by Nasiruddin al-Khattab. Riyadh, Saudi Arabia, and London: Darussalam, 2002.

Menocal, Maria Rosa. *The Ornament of the World, How Muslims, Jews, and Christians Created a Culture of Tolerance in Medieval Spain.* Boston: Little, Brown, 2002.

Nasr, Seyyed Hossein. *The Heart of Islam: Enduring Values for Humanity.* San Francisco: HarperSan Francisco, 2002.

Rāb'ah al-'Adawīyah. *Doorkeeper of the Heart: Versions of Rabi'a.* Translated by Charles Upton. Putney, VT: Threshold Books, 1988.

Renard, John. *In the Footsteps of Muhammad: Understanding the Islamic Experience.* New York: Paulist Press, 1992.

————, ed. *Windows on the House of Islam: Muslim Sources on Spirituality and Religious Life.* Berkeley: University of California Press, 1998.

Sachedina, Abdulaziz Abdulhussein. *The Islamic Roots of Democratic Pluralism.* New York and Oxford, England: Oxford University Press, 2001.

Sardar, Ziauddin and Zafar Abbas Malik. *Muhammad for Beginners.* Cambridge, England: Icon Books, 2004.

Schuon, Frithjof. *Understanding Islam.* Bloomington, IN: World Wisdom Books, 1998.

————. *The Transcendent Unity of Religions.* Wheaton, IL: The Theosophical Publishing House, 1993.

Siddiqi, Muhammad Zubair. *Hadith Literature: Its Origin, Development and Special Features.* Edited by Abdal Hakim Murad. Cambridge, England: The Islamic Texts Society, 1993.

Al-Tirmidhi, Abi Iassa Muhammed. *Characteristics of the Prophet Muhammad.* Translation and commentary by Bahaa Addin Ibrahim Ahmed Shalaby. Cairo, Egypt: Dar Al Manarah, 2003.

Wolfe, Michael, ed. *Taking Back Islam: American Muslims Reclaim Their Faith.* Emmaus, PA: Rodale, 2002.

———. *One Thousand Roads to Mecca: Ten Centuries of Travelers Writing about the Muslim Pilgrimage.* New York: Grove Press 1997.

**WEB SITES**

Encyclopedia of the Orient

http://lexicorient.com/i-e.o/2b.htm

Islam

http://www.teachingaboutreligion.org/Backdrop&Context/islam.htm

Islam and Islamic Studies Resources

http://www.arches.uga.edu/~godlas/

Islam: Empire of Faith

http://www.pbs.org/empires/islam/

Islamicity: The Holy Quran

http://www.islamicity.com/mosque/quran/

Muslim Heritage

http://www.muslimheritage.com

Muslim Life in America

http://usinfo.state.gov/products/pubs/muslimlife/homepage.htm

Muslims the Facts

http://www.newint.org/issue345/facts.htm

Religion & Ethics: Islam

http://www.bbc.co.uk/religion/religions/islam/index.shtml

# SOURCE NOTES

Most English translations of the Quran are from Muhammad Asad, *The Message of the Quran*. Gibraltar: Dar al-Andulus, 1980.

**CHAPTER ONE:**

p. 21: "Do not *worry—he is not lost to you!*" Reynold A. Nicholson, Mathnawi of Jalal al-Din Rumi (Gibb Memorial Trust, 1990), vol. 4, line 976.

p. 22: "Take this boy back to his country . . ." Martin Lings, *Muhammad: His Life Based on the Earliest Sources* (Rochester, VT: Inner Traditions International, 1983), p. 30.

pp. 24–25: "If you placed the sun in my right hand . . ." Yusuf Islam, *The Life of the Last Prophet* (Chicago: Mountain of Light, 2001), p. 45.

pp. 25–26: "Until today there was no face on earth . . ." http://www.islamonline.com, Muslim Profiles.

p. 26: "God, guide them on the right path . . ." Islam, *The Life of the Last Prophet*, p. 57.

p. 30: "Let her go her way . . ." Lings, *Muhammad*, p. 123.

p. 36: "Did he not cut the sleeve from his coat . . ." Annemarie Schimmel, *And Muhammad Is His Messanger: The Veneration of the Prophet in Islamic Piety*, (Chapel Hill: University of North Carolina Press, 1985), p. 81.

p. 37: "You are the daughter of the prophet Aaron, . . ." http://www.islamonline.com, Wives of the Prophet.

**CHAPTER TWO:**

p. 43: "I have been given the authority over you, . . ." Ziauddin Sardar and Zafar Abbas Malik, *Muhammad for Beginners,* (Cambridge, England: Icon Books, 2004) p. 68.

p. 59: "Democracy does not ensure justice. . . ." Khaled Abou El Fadl, *Islam and the Challenge of Democracy,* (Princeton, NJ: Princeton University Press, 2004), p. 6.

**CHAPTER THREE:**

p. 78: "Just as medicaments are composed . . ." Abu Hamid al-Ghazālī, *Deliverance from Error: Five Key Texts Including His Spiritual Autobiography, Al Munqidh min al-Dalal* (Louisville, KY: Fons Vitae, 2004), p. 29.

p. 81: "Bringing about a just reconciliation between . . ." Muhammad Ali Alkhuli, *The Light of Islam,* (Amman: Alfalah House, 1990), p. 123.

p. 84: "For centuries, the pilgrimage used to be the annual . . ." Feisal Abdul Rauf, *What's Right with Islam,* (San Francisco: HarperSan Francisco, 2004), p. 115.

pp. 84–85: "The pilgrimage is a prefiguration of the inward journey . . ." Frithjof Schuon, *Understanding Islam* (Bloomington, IN: World Wisdom Books, 1998), p. 33.

**CHAPTER FOUR:**

p. 87: "The psychological war you wage within yourself . . ." Faisal Abdul Rauf, *Islam, a Sacred Law: What Every Muslim Should Know about Shariah,* (Brattleboro, VT: Qiblah Books, 1999), p. 72.

pp. 88–90: "The Quran is not a linear narration. . . ." From an interview with Hamza Yusuf Hanson, *Muhammad: Legacy of the Prophet,* http://www.pbs.org/muhammad/transcripts/hanson.html accessed December 14, 2005.

p. 99: "The Prophet has said, . . ." Jonathan Bloom and Sheila Blair, *Islam, Empire of Faith,* (London: BBC, 2001), p. 173.

**CHAPTER FIVE:**

pp. 108–110: "The convergence of youth sub-culture, elitism, . . ." Asef Bayat, "From Amr Diab to Amr Khaled," *Al-Ahram Weekly Online,* http://weekly.ahram.org.eg/2003/639/fe1/htm, accessed December 20, 2005.

p. 111: "I would rather live as a Muslim in the west . . ." Jack O'Sullivan, "If you hate the west, emigrate to a Muslim country," *The Guardian* (London), October 8, 2001.

p. 111: "Many Muslims regard the form of government . . ." Rauf, *What's Right with Islam* p. 118.

# INDEX

# ABOUT THE AUTHOR

**CLAIRE ALKOUATLI** is a freelance writer and editor living in Jeddah, Saudi Arabia, with her husband and young child. She has contributed several articles to the travel section of Canada's national newspaper, the *Globe and Mail*, and her essays have appeared in publications as diverse as *Parabola* magazine, *Arabian Woman* magazine, and *The Bangladesh Today* newspaper. In November 2002, she wrote an essay entitled "Traveling the Road toward Islam" for Avalon's anthology *Bare Your Soul: The Thinking Girl's Guide to Enlightenment.*

Claire was the executive editor of *Blue*, an adventure travel magazine based in New York City, from 1998 to 2002. During her time at the helm, *Blue* won several awards, including honors from *FOLIO* and *Life*.

For the last ten years, Claire has traveled on and off throughout the Muslim world, including Egypt, Syria, Oman, and Bangladesh. During her time spent in Muslim countries, Claire became drawn to Islam and accepted the religion in November 2001.